About Jack Patterson and
DEAD IN THE WATER

In *Dead in the Water*, Jack Patterson accurately captures the action-packed saga of what could be a real-life college football scandal. The sordid details will leave readers flipping through the pages as fast as a hurry-up offense."

WITHDRAWN

- **Mark Schlabach**
ESPN college sports columnist and
co-author of Called to Coach *and*
Heisman: The Man Behind the Trophy

"Jack's storytelling feels as natural as James Patterson's, and the short-chapter setup is the literary answer to Lay's potato chips: you just want one more and before you know it, you've gone through the whole thing.

- **David Bashore**
The Times-News, Twin Falls, ID

"Jack Patterson does a fantastic job at keeping you engaged and interested. I look forward to more from this talented author."

-*Aaron Patterson*
bestselling author of SWEET DREAMS

DEAD SHOT

"Small town life in southern Idaho might seem quaint and idyllic to some. But when local newspaper reporter Cal Murphy begins to uncover a series of strange deaths that are linked to a sticky spider web of deception, the lid on the peaceful town is blown wide open. Told with all the energy and bravado of an old pro, first-timer Jack Patterson hits one out of the park his first time at bat with *Dead Shot*. It's that good."

- Vincent Zandri
bestselling author of THE REMAINS

"You can tell Jack knows what it's like to live in the newspaper world, but with *Dead Shot*, he's proven that he also can write one heck of a murder mystery. With a clever plot and characters you badly want to succeed, he is on his way to becoming a new era James Patterson."

- Josh Katzowitz
NFL writer for CBSSports.com
& author of Sid Gillman: Father of the Passing Game

"Patterson has a mean streak about a mile wide and puts his two main characters through quite a horrible ride, which makes for good reading."

- Richard D., reader

DEAD LINE

"This book kept me on the edge of my seat the whole time. I didn't really want to put it down. Jack Patterson has hooked me. I'll be back for more."

"Like a John Grisham novel, from the very start I was pulled right into the story and couldn't put the book down. It was as if I personally knew and cared about what happened to each of the main characters. Every chapter ended with so much excitement and suspense I had to continue to read until I learned how it ended, even though it kept me up until 3:00 A.M.

THE WARREN OMISSIONS

"What can be more fascinating than a super high concept novel that reopens the conspiracy behind the JFK assassination while the threat of a global world war rests in the balance? With his new novel, *The Warren Omissions*, former journalist turned bestselling author Jack Patterson proves he just might be the next worthy successor to Vince Flynn."

Other titles by Jack Patterson

Cal Murphy Thriller series
Dead Shot
Dead Line
Better off Dead
Dead in the Water
Dead Man's Curve
Dead and Gone
Dead Wrong
Dead Man's Land

James Flynn Thriller series
The Warren Omissions
Imminent Threat

DEAD IN THE WATER

A Novel

JACK PATTERSON

Dead in the Water
© Copyright 2014 Jack Patterson

This novel is a work of fiction. Names, characters, places, and incidents either are the product of the author's imagination or are used fictitiously. Any resemblance to actual persons, living or dead, events, or locales is entirely coincidental.

Print ISBN: 978-1-938848-55-1
eBook ISBN: 978-1-938848-49-0

First Print Edition 2014

Cover Design by Dan Pitts

Published in the United States of America
Hangman Books
Boise Idaho 83713

For Don Brown

CHAPTER 1

TRE'VELL BAKER CLIMBED OUT of Dominique Dixon's rusted out Civic and popped the hatchback. He grabbed his football gear and backpack before thanking his friend for the ride.

"Same time, same place Monday?" Dixon asked.

Baker nodded. "I wouldn't miss it."

Baker never missed it. Saint-Parran High's most sought-after recruits in nearly two decades rode home together after every practice. It was a rare Friday night without a football game as Saint-Parran prepared for the upcoming Louisiana high school state playoffs.

Baker sat down and continued his routine, awaiting the arrival of his youngest brother's school bus. Within five minutes, the bus appeared and began applying its squeaky brakes. The door flung open and Jarvis hopped off. He smiled at his big brother before racing to him for a hug.

"Hey, little man," Baker said. "How was school today?"

"It was great," Jarvis responded.

"How come?"

"Fourth down and the game was tied," Jarvis began his tale. "We needed a touchdown. Mr. Bixby said it was time to come in, so we only had one more play. Who do you think

9

they threw the ball to?"

"Do you even need to ask?"

"Randall threw the ball into the end zone and I dove and caught it to win the game."

Baker looked down at his little brother, whose face beamed with pride as he waited for a compliment.

"You're going to be better than me one day," Baker said, rubbing his brother's head.

With a half-mile walk ahead of them, Baker helped Jarvis shed his backpack and added it to his own burden. The cypress trees cast a thick canopy over the dirt road, a canopy that was already thinning as fall neared its annual secession to Old Man Winter. Sunlight danced between the shadows while Jarvis shared more excitement of a day in first grade. Playground conquests and compliments from the teacher highlighted their daily walks—and today was no different.

It wouldn't be long before Baker would leave Saint-Parran, and Nikko, his thirteen-year-old brother, would assume the role of caring for their youngest sibling. Baker felt time marching toward him without any way to dodge it, no matter how deft he was at escaping.

When it came to eluding would-be tacklers, Baker held a special knack. At 6 feet 4 inches tall, and 235 pounds, Baker presented a healthy-sized target for quarterbacks. Though his size alone wasn't what made him one of the most prized recruits in the entire state of Louisiana. No, it was his speed and agility that did that. His forty-yard dash time of 4.4 seconds blistered most of his competition. When Baker's team was on offense, the plan was simple: get Baker the ball. His whirling moves coupled with his speed and size made him nearly impossible to defend. And it was for such talent that he would be leaving Saint-Parran, hopefully bringing his entire family with him.

But the likelihood of his mother and brothers joining him seemed slim in the wake of recent events.

A few short weeks ago, Baker and Dixon had taken an official recruiting trip to Bryant University. The young university in northern Alabama had taken the college football world by storm. Less than twenty years ago, the nephew of legendary Alabama coach Bear Bryant, Andrew Bryant, founded Bryant University. As a youngster, Andrew wanted to play for Alabama more than anything in the world—like the majority of the boys who grow up in the state—and made it his mission in life to do so. When his uncle didn't offer him a scholarship, Andrew enrolled and walked on. After just one practice, Bear Bryant cut his nephew. Instead of growing bitter, Andrew decided to get even. By the time he was forty, he had amassed a fortune so sizeable that he landed at number twenty on Forbes' list of "Richest People in America." While he contributed plenty of money to charity, what Andrew really wanted was to spend his money to create a university, one with a football team that would upset the balance of power in the football-crazed state of Alabama. Huntsville emerged as the best city in which to start such an institution. The university was state of the art and had garnered plenty of academic acclaim in a short period of time. The athletic facilities dazzled and the coaches sold the opportunity to build something great—and maybe even win a championship. Dixon fell for the pitch. Baker did, too, but not without some extra coaxing.

Openly spurning Louisiana State for a school in nearby Alabama had done little to endear Saint-Parran's dynamic duo to the locals. Once they graduated, their hometown support was sure to all but disappear. But Baker didn't care—and neither did Dixon.

Every day in practice, the two fiercely competed against each other. Dixon, a defensive back, made Baker's life miserable. Dixon defended each pass thrown to Baker as if it were the last play of the Super Bowl. They fed off each other. Pitting two of the best players in the state against each other only served to spur them on. They loved the competition—yet they wanted nothing more than to play together at the next level. And they wanted to go somewhere that made them happy, not stay in a town they would rather forget and leave behind.

It wasn't that Saint-Parran was full of bad people—in fact, it was barely full of people at all. If it weren't for some of the best fishing in Louisiana, Saint-Parran would likely never exist. It would simply be known as the area near Devil's Fork Bayou. But good fishing attracted plenty of retired snowbirds and wealthy men in search of a trophy fish or a gator hide.

Baker ended up in Saint-Parran after his parents moved the family there from New Orleans. Why his mother never returned baffled Baker. His father left them when Baker was five, leaving his mother, Lanette, pregnant and penniless. His mother had a couple of live-in boyfriends that resulted in the additions of Tashawn, who was now eleven, and Jarvis, to the family. To make ends meet, Lanette grabbed every shift she could at Lagniappe Café off Highway 1 where what little action in Saint-Parran occurred. It was a dingy dive but patronized by mostly generous tippers, who kept Lanette and her family fed and clothed. For several years, Baker begged his mother to leave and search for employment elsewhere, but she refused. Her hope of a real life, one that didn't mean scraping by, had all but vanished.

But Baker saw a way out for his mother when college coaches began parading through their three-bedroom slat-board house that sat just several feet from the edge of the creeping waters of Devil's Fork Bayou. Baker dreamed of playing professionally one day, but he knew better than to bank on it. He saw opportunity in front him—a chance to help his mother and brothers escape an endless cycle of poverty—and he seized it. Whenever a coach entered his home, Baker asked the questions. He showed mild interest in how coaches intended to use him in their offense or in what academic offerings the school had. However, his real measuring stick for choosing a school came down to who wanted him more—as in, who wanted to give him the most.

Baker knew it was wrong. The National Collegiate Athletic Association—the NCAA —forbade such "gifts." Tuition with room and board was enough. At most schools, such a scholarship package was equivalent to two hundred thousand dollars—a seemingly fair trade for playing football for four or five seasons. But Baker knew the scholarships meant nothing and he'd heard from others that it wasn't the only thing schools would offer him, whether it was against the rules or not. So with a wink, Baker always asked the coaches what else they could do for him. Most coaches gave some standard line about keeping him safe and helping prepare him for the real world. Baker always scoffed at such comments. He lived in the real world and he'd always stayed safe. Those promises didn't interest him—and most coaches sensed it right away.

The Bryant University coaches were different. They knew exactly what he was asking about—and they laid out a nice package. Lanette would have a new home, a car, and a job at the university bookstore as a manager. They praised her ability as a waitress and how she handled a grumpy customer while they were dining at her café. They noted that her customer service skills were why they thought she would make a great manager. The idea of caring for his mom in this way sold Baker on attending Bryant University.

In the weeks after they announced a verbal commitment to Bryant University, Baker grew uneasy over how the coaches broke the rules with such flippancy. All it would take is one disgruntled player to turn on them before the NCAA launched an investigation and discovered the type of impropriety that would result in heavy sanctions to the football program. Maybe the NCAA would take away scholarships, strip victories, or ban the game from playing in bowl games or worse—receive the dreaded death penalty that shut down the program. Nevertheless, Baker decided to take an official visit there with Dixon to assuage his fears. The reward would be worth it if the risk didn't seem too detrimental to his future career and potential earnings should he make it to the NFL.

Despite their friendship, Baker kept the full extent of Bryant's offer to himself. He didn't want jealousy to come between he and Dixon when the real joy of this opportunity was getting to play football together in college. Dixon's loose lips already shared that Bryant coaches promised him a car and a sizeable stipend under the table each week. There was also a summer internship at a car dealership that paid above average and included a flexible schedule. They both understood that deal—a healthy paycheck whether or not you showed up for work. Dixon saw a way to better his future; Baker wanted a better future for his entire family.

Yet during their recruiting visit, Baker saw something,

something terrible. He wasn't supposed to see it, but it was the kind of thing he couldn't un-see or un-know. Baker was goofing around on his smart phone—one given to him a few months earlier by a Bryant University booster—and happened to record a video of it. Nobody knew he knew, except Dixon. On the way home, Baker showed the video to Dixon. Its contents scared Dixon so much that he suggested that maybe they should look elsewhere. Baker felt conflicted, knowing that such a decision meant his family may not get all they were dreaming of—and neither would Dixon. But Baker had to draw the line somewhere, and Bryant University had obliterated the line. For Baker, Bryant had committed the unpardonable sin.

The weight of Baker's decision rested heavily upon him. It was almost all he thought about since he and Dixon reneged on their commitment to play at Bryant. *Where would he go? What would happen to his family? Could his brothers make it out of the bayou with their heads still screwed on straight?* There were no answers, only wild speculation that kept Baker up at night and left him unfocused during the day.

That's why the adventures of a first grader were a welcome break for Baker. Jarvis was young but he could spin some yarn, making a mundane trip across the monkey bars seem as exciting as Vasco da Gamma circumnavigating Africa.

"Did you talk to any girls today?" Baker asked.

"Ewww. No way," Jarvis said. "One of them tried to talk to me, but I told her I'd rather kiss a dead fish."

Baker laughed. "Speakin' of fish, you wanna do some fishin' before mom gets home?"

Jarvis nodded with exuberance. He darted ahead to the dilapidated shed that held all the family's fishing gear.

Baker knew he'd miss fishing in the bayou. It was a sanctuary of sorts, a level playing field for everyone casting their bait into the dark waters and hoping to pull out a tale-worthy fish. There were no expectations on Baker here. No touchdowns to score, no coaches to impress, no dreams hanging in the balance. Just a kid and his rod and some bait. Compared to fishing, everything else in Baker's life seemed complicated.

By the time Baker reached the family's run-down dock, Jarvis was already sitting on one of the rickety boards and baiting his hook. Baker checked his little brother's attempt to secure a chicken liver on his hook before letting him toss it into the water. The chicken liver wasn't going anywhere without a firm bite from a channel catfish lurking in the murky waters below.

Baker sat down and took a deep breath. He smiled and rubbed Jarvis on the head.

"You're all right, you know that?" Baker said.

Jarvis nodded and smile, yet kept his gaze on the water, waiting for a strike from some unlucky catfish.

Baker looked up at the trees and the sky, which was quickly fading from bright blue to hues of light red. If not for the shrill chirps from the short-billed Dowitchers, the only audible sound would've been the faint current pushing the bayou's waters along.

Baker looked at Jarvis with pride. He knew his little brother was special and was going to be the best athlete in the family one day. Yet he was unsure just how much of a chance Jarvis would have, stuck in the bayou his whole life. Just like the ecosystem surrounding him, life in the bayou was fragile. One bad hurricane or one failed fishing outfitter and Saint-Parran might join a list of growing ghost towns deep within Louisiana's bayou. And then what? Could their mother adapt? Where would she go? How would she provide for her boys? He couldn't help but feel guilty over his decision to spurn Bryant University as he looked at his baby brother. Maybe he could change his mind, restore his original commitment—if the offer still stood. But he just couldn't. Baker couldn't shake what he saw and it went against every fiber of his being. Bryant University was a dirty program with dirty coaches. And if the program's indiscretions ever drew the watchful eye of the NCAA, Baker knew his mom and brothers would be on the first bus back to the bayou.

So much for a few peaceful moments fishing.

Baker snapped out of his funk when a splash in the water led to an excited yelp from Jarvis. Baker scrambled to his feet and steadied Jarvis' rod as they fought a feisty catfish dancing beneath the water. Jarvis slowly reeled in the fish. Baker grabbed the net and scooped the fish with it. The catfish twitched and flopped on the deck as Jarvis stared wide-eyed at his catch.

"I think that's the biggest one I've ever caught!" Jarvis said.

Baker smiled and gave Jarvis a one-armed hug. The catfish looked about eighteen inches long, but Baker was sure that by the time Jarvis arrived at school on Monday and began retelling his exploits, the fish would grow an additional eighteen inches.

For a brief moment, Baker forgot all about his troubles and the decisions bearing on him. Sheer joy consumed his thoughts as he watched Jarvis dance delicately on the shaky dock. It was the last thing Baker thought about before a bullet exploded into the back of his head and sent him headlong into the bayou.

CHAPTER 2

IT HAD BEEN TWO YEARS since Cal Murphy accepted a job at the *Atlanta Journal-Constitution* and moved east. Becoming an enterprise reporter for the sports department meant more freedom that he'd ever had in his career. Freedom to chase down fragile leads. Freedom to pursue injustices that would otherwise slip under the radar. Freedom to explore the kind of stories that attracted him to journalism in the first place. It breathed new life into Cal as a journalist. Meanwhile, the rest of his life was on hold, stifled by the kind of cruelty dished out exclusively by the likes of Mother Nature, acts of God, and Lady Unluck.

When Cal proposed to his girlfriend, Kelly Mendoza, he sensed a change in his life. For once, things were going his way. He had the type of job he always dreamed of—and now the girl, too. Just before proposing to Kelly, Cal concluded an investigative report that rocked the NFL, revealing a performance enhancing drug cover-up that shook up the league's policies and landscape of the cheating teams. It also created an intense bidding war for his services as a writer. To top it off, Kelly said yes—and they were off on an adventure in the deep South, this time together.

Cal was mildly shocked at Kelly's eagerness to join him

without a job of her own. Kelly had worked for the Associated Press as a photographer in southern California but left knowing there were no openings in Atlanta. Cal figured it would be easy for someone as talented as her to find a job somewhere, if not as a freelance photographer. During their first year in Atlanta, she managed to pick up a few jobs here and there, but nothing permanent—and nothing that paid much of anything. Cal watched as it sent Kelly spiraling into depression.

After a year, Kelly came to Cal with an idea, something to give her purpose since her photography career seemed to be disappearing.

"Cal, I don't know if I can do this anymore," she said.

"Do what?"

"Boredom. It's driving me crazy."

"What do you propose we do about it?"

"I want a baby."

Anxious to become a father, Cal agreed. But it wasn't long before the couple realized something was wrong. A trip to the fertility specialist confirmed their worst fear: Kelly would likely never get pregnant.

"There's only one procedure that's had much success correcting your condition, Kelly," the doctor told them.

"What are our chances if it works?" Cal asked.

"If the procedure goes well, couples get pregnant within a year about eighty percent of the time."

"So is there any downside to this?" Kelly asked.

"It's an elective surgery and is rarely covered by your insurance."

"Is that a problem?" Cal asked.

"No, but it's an expensive surgery." He slid a paper across the desk that detailed the costs.

They left the doctor's office searching for ideas for how they could come up with an extra $40,000.

Cal calculated that even if Kelly took a job at a small newspaper, it would still take two years before she could earn enough money for the surgery. And then there was always the gruesome reality that the surgery might not work. It was too much of a risk in his mind, too long to put their life on hold. Cal wasn't sure how much longer Kelly would last before the dark depression brooding over her stole her last shred of joy. He needed another solution—a quick one.

As he pondered where he could come up with such a large amount of money so quickly, Cal received a call from Barry Anderson, one of his college buddies.

"Barry Anderson? To what do I owe the pleasure of this phone call?"

"It's been far too long, Cal."

"So, what are you doing these days?"

"I'm not developing a reputation as the best investigative sports journalist in the business, that's for sure."

Cal laughed. "Don't believe everything you hear."

"I don't, but I was wondering if you could help me with a book I'm working on. I need some background on your story about the L.A. Stars a while back."

Cal didn't mind sharing notes with Anderson, who'd been a good friend in college. Though they had spoken in recent years, Anderson's call testified to the strength of their relationship.

"Before I let you go, I've got a question for you," Cal said.

"Shoot."

"I'd like to get into writing books myself. It's a long story, but I need to come up with a large amount of money and fast—and I think a book deal would be a great way to do that."

"Gambling again, Cal?"

Cal chuckled. "No, I quit betting and playing beer pong our senior year."

"You were a drag that last year of college."

"Seriously, do you think you can help me?"

Anderson gave Cal a few names of literary agents, thanked him for the information and wished him good luck.

Cal reached out to several literary agents but heard nothing. He was almost ready to begin looking for a higher paying job elsewhere when one of the literary agents he'd spoken with a few weeks before contacted him.

"Mr. Murphy?"

"Yes?" Cal answered.

"This is Mike Nicholson from Nicholson & Associates. We spoke briefly about your interest in writing some sports-related books."

"Yes, I remember. How are you?"

"I'm doing well, thanks. And yourself?"

"I'm all right. Still wracking my brain for a book idea that could get published."

"Well, I think I found a potential one for you and wanted to see if you were interested."

"Oh? Tell me about it." Cal sat down at his desk and pulled out a note pad, ready to hear the big idea.

"While college football recruiting has become a hot commodity as it pertains to reader interest among newspapers and sports websites, very few books are being written about it. And for good reason—recruiting coverage builds toward signing day and then it's over."

"Yes, I know," Cal said. "I hate covering recruiting. A

bunch of seventeen- and eighteen-year-old boys who are indecisive and easily swayed make for a maddening few months of work."

"Very true. However, there is a side to recruiting that hasn't been covered much—the dark side. And I've got a publisher who wants a book on the dark side of recruiting."

"What exactly do you mean by that?"

"I mean, he wants a book that exposes the dirty tactics and cheating ways of major universities. However, he'll settle for the story of one school."

"One school? Everybody does it. Why just one?"

"In this case, the publisher thinks he sees potential in a story brewing down in Louisiana that could make for one heckuva book on recruiting."

"And what story is that?"

"The murder of Louisiana five-star recruit Tre'vell Baker."

"Recruits getting murdered before signing day isn't common but it has happened before."

"True, but there's something about this story that doesn't pass the smell test. For starters, the Baker kid was committed to Bryant University before suddenly reneging on his commitment. Then he winds up dead a week later after rumors emerged that he was going to Alabama instead."

"Perhaps that's just coincidence?"

"Coincidence? I thought I was talking to Cal Murphy, journalist extraordinaire who's found enough dirt on sports figures in the past few years to fill a pig farm's mud pit."

"You are, Mr. Nicholson. But conspiracy theories abound in college football. And even when you know a school is cheating, the NCAA struggles to prove it."

"Sure. But cheating is one thing—murder is another."

"What makes you so sure that the Baker kid's murder is directly tied to dirty recruiting?"

"The publisher said he just has a hunch."

"And who's the publisher?"

"I'm not at liberty to say, but let's just say he's willing to pay you a handsome advance if this story is true."

"Define handsome."

"Nothing definitive yet, but he said it will be six figures."

Cal gasped but remained quiet.

"Cal? Are you there?" Nicholson asked.

"Yes, I'm here," he answered.

"Well, what do you think?"

"I think I'll talk to my editor about it and get back with you."

Cal hung up and tried to temper his excitement. He then ran into the kitchen to tell Kelly.

He then spent the next few minutes trying to temper her excitement as they hugged and dreamed of the possibilities.

"Nothing is for certain, but I'm going to convince my editor to let me go down to Louisiana and check it out," Cal said.

Kelly smiled and gave him a few more encouraging words before he left the house for work.

***

When Cal arrived at the offices of *The Atlanta Journal-Constitution*—more commonly known as *The AJC*—Jim Gatlin was standing outside and taking the final drag of a cigarette. Cal shot him a disapproving glance before Gatlin tossed the butt down and mashed it into the sidewalk.

"I'm trying to quit," Gatlin said. "Cut me some slack,

will ya? It's Friday."

Cal smiled and nodded. He never once said a word to Gatlin about his smoking habit. Such browbeating toward smokers in the newspaper business would make Cal the most hated man in the newsroom. It was an acceptable mechanism to cope with all the daily stress associated with the job. Alcohol was also acceptable, though less so on the clock. However, Cal's mere presence as a non-smoker seemed to extract Gatlin's guilt. It was an uneasiness Cal wished didn't exist between him and his boss.

"So, you got any leads on any good stories today?" Gatlin asked as they strode toward the elevator.

Cal nodded. "I think so."

"Good. We need a good enterprise piece to fill up some space for the Thanksgiving issue in less than two weeks."

"Not sure if it's that good of a lead," Cal answered as he pushed the button for the fourth floor.

"Try me."

"Heard about a five-star college football recruit murdered in the bayou and my source tells me that foul play was involved." Cal flinched as he stretched the truth.

"Who was the kid?"

"Tre'vell Baker from Saint-Parran."

"Oh, that receiver kid? I've seen highlights of him on Youtube. He's a beast."

"Yeah, well, he's dead now, and my source has good reason to believe it's related to football."

"I like it. We could go with the headline of 'The Dark Underbelly of College Football' or something like that."

"Haven't you used that before?"

They exited the elevator before Gatlin shot him a look.

"Are you trying to get on my bad side today?" Gatlin

asked.

Cal smiled. "Do you even have a good side?"

"OK, fine. Go check it out. I wish it were somewhere in Georgia or Alabama instead of the godforsaken swamp that is Louisiana."

"Gotta cover 'Dixie like the Dew,' right?"

"Sure—but you better come back with something, dark underbelly or not. Got it?"

Cal nodded and headed for his desk. He needed to do some more research—and book a flight for New Orleans.

CHAPTER 3

HUGH SANDERS HUNCHED LOW and peered across the horizon. There weren't many activities that approached Sanders' love for fishing around Devil's Fork Bayou, but duck hunting was a formidable rival. As autumn settled in, Sanders enjoyed exchanging his fishing rod and boat for a shotgun and a duck blind. He nestled low to the ground in an effort to maintain his advantage on the targets approaching. Then in one smooth action, he hoisted his Browning Gold shotgun into the air and took aim.

Blam! Blam! Blam!

Splash!

Once the duck hit the water, Roxie, Sanders' Labrador Retriever took off in the direction of the downed bird.

"Go get her, girl!" Sanders shouted as a huge grin spread across his face.

"Ain't nothin' like it nowhere," he mumbled to himself as he watched Roxie gently secure the duck in her mouth and begin swimming back toward the blind.

Yet Sanders muttered the same expression for plenty of other joys in his life—reeling in a large bass, selling a fleet of cars to a business, and after every Alabama touchdown. To Sanders, these were the simple things in life, but they were also non-negotiable. Losing was not an option. He'd do just about anything to win. *Anything.*

Sanders welcomed Roxie back and retrieved the pintail duck from her mouth.

"That's a good girl," he said as he rubbed her head.

Four mallards and two pintails. Time to call it a day.

Sanders didn't quit until he bagged the limit. Whenever he went hunting though, it was a foregone conclusion that he would get everything he could legally. Sanders only pulled the trigger three times because he liked shooting his gun, not because he needed the extra two shots to kill his prey.

He checked his watch. It was still early, but he had a full day ahead of him, one that included a church service and a meeting with Dominique Dixon to convince him to become a football player for the University of Alabama.

Sanders collected his gear and headed for his truck. He struggled to get anywhere quickly. *Maybe I should've held off the buffet last night. Thank God for belts.* His good looks long since gone, Sanders paused to stare at his 58-year-old face in the truck's side mirrors. *Beauty's fleeting but power isn't,* he thought to himself as he raked his thinning gray hair over to one side.

Slightly out of breath, Sanders stowed all his gear just before his phone rang. He recognized the number right away.

"Hello, Coach. How are you on this fine mornin'?"

It was Dick Raymond, head coach of the University of Alabama's football team. Raymond publicly rebuked boosters' involvement in the recruiting process. But that was all for show. Privately, he had a dozen Alabama boosters on his speed dial and employed them to add a little sugar to his sales pitching to play at the school. This elite corps of boosters would drop everything to help. It was their way of contributing to the program beyond money. Raymond believed it was the little things that made the difference; his three championship rings proved he knew what he was talking about. When he preached this same message at alumni and booster meetings across the state of Alabama, everyone said amen with more than just their pocketbooks. They would do anything for Raymond. Hugh Sanders was no different.

Sanders knew the purpose of Raymond's call: to secure Dixon's commitment to the school. Alabama lost two games the previous season and failed to win a conference championship, far below the standards Raymond set when he first began coaching there. It was a title or bust. And last season was a bust due to an inexperienced secondary that gave up passing yards by the truckloads. They needed to shore up their defense. They needed Dixon.

Receiving such calls from Raymond made Sanders feel important. He'd always loved Alabama football, but never did he dream he would be speaking regularly with the head of the program, much less helping secure star recruits.

"Don't worry, Coach," Sanders said. "He's gonna be wearin' crimson and white next fall. I guarantee it."

Sanders hung up and jumped into his truck. He needed to wash up before he got his hands dirty again.

***

Sanders fidgeted in his seat as Father Benoit prayed and began his homily. As far back as he could remember, Sanders attended church on Sundays. It was a Sanders family tradition. No excuses. Once when Sanders was nine, he contracted a nasty virus that kept him out of school for three days and made him miss his football game on Saturday. But when Sunday morning arrived, Sanders was in church along with his cold sweat and aches. Try as he might, Sanders couldn't get out of the habit. While he considered his true sanctuary to be Bryant-Denny Stadium in Tuscaloosa on Saturdays, any building with a cross would suffice for Sundays.

St. Anne's Catholic Church in Saint-Parran met Sanders' criteria. He would've gone elsewhere if possible, but it was the only church in the parish. Despite his aversion to kneeling, sitting and standing—positions he regularly took throughout every Alabama football game—Sanders walked into St. Anne's with a smile on his face. He usually attended a large Baptist church in Birmingham when he was home running his multi-million dollar car dealership. But when he had a chance to get in some extra fishing and hunting, Sanders piloted his PC-12 to Saint-Parran and his second home in the bayou. Most of his wealthy peers would have preferred to purchase a second home on a beach somewhere, but not Sanders. Sitting in the sand and reading a book was not his idea of a relaxing time.

Sanders caught himself paying attention as Father Benoit extoled the virtues of honesty.

"In Proverbs, King Solomon shares a simple truth: 'A faithful witness will not lie: but a deceitful witness uttereth a lie,'" Father Benoit said.

Sanders squirmed in his seat. He was no liar, but he didn't mind stretching the truth—as long as it was for a good cause. He figured some kids needed a little more coaxing to go to Alabama and that in the long run an education at the finest university on the planet with undoubtedly the best football team would benefit them more than they might realize. Bending and exaggerating the truth were helpful tactics in a game with life-altering implications. It's not really lying if everyone was doing it. Sanders decided not to ponder the scripture for too long before Father Benoit read his mind and called him out by name.

Once the service ended, Sanders hustled out the door and to his truck. He didn't want to keep Dominique Dixon waiting.

***

All respectable business in Saint-Parran occurred at Lagniappe Café. It was the meeting place of choice for Sanders, who asked Dixon to meet him there that afternoon. Sanders ordered a coffee and waited for his guest. He scanned the room for any new additions to the wall. Nothing new. Just the same old faded out newspaper clippings from glory years gone by.

Fifteen minutes after one, Dixon strode through the front door. He wore a black hoodie and grey sweatpants with the number eighty-one stitched on the left side. Sanders gave a little head nod to Dixon, who walked slowly toward his table.

"Have a seat," Sanders said, gesturing toward the empty chair in front of him.

Dixon sat down and didn't say a word.

"I wanted to offer my condolences about Tre'vell," Sanders began. "He was a class act."

Dixon stared down at the table and nodded.

"He was," Dixon said.

"It's crazy to think someone is runnin' around the woods and shootin' at people."

"You ain't kiddin'."

"Look, I'm sorry. I don't meant to bring up bad memories. I'd heard you two were close—"

"We were tight. But it's no big deal. He's gone now and there's nothin' we can do about it."

"Does the sheriff know who did it?"

Dixon scowled at Sanders. "Are we here to talk about Tre'vell or me?"

"Sorry. Yes, we're here to talk about you. So, how do you feel about becomin' part of the Alabama family?"

"I don't know. I haven't thought about it too much."

"Haven't thought about it? You mean, you haven't pondered what it would be like to play for the greatest football program in all of the land?"

Dixon snickered. "Look, I know you probably bleed crimson and white, but it's not that clear cut for me. Besides, Tre'vell and I made a pact to go to the same school, no matter where it was. I can't keep that promise now, but I still want to honor his memory wherever I go."

Sanders looked down, unsure of how to proceed. Though he'd only met Tre'vell Baker once, Sanders was sure he was well on his way to playing for Alabama after he reneged on his commitment to Bryant University. Baker's death actually created a twinge of pain for him as well.

"Look, I'm very sorry for your loss," Sanders began. "I met Tre'vell once at a camp in Tuscaloosa and he seemed like a great kid. And I can't imagine what this all feels like for you. I know it's not easy. But don't let this paralyze your decision-making process. There are only so many scholarships available at Alabama—and you're at the top of Coach Raymond's list. But if you decide to go elsewhere or drag your feet, that scholarship may not be there by the time you have to make a decision."

Dixon nodded.

A waitress topped off Sanders' coffee and placed a menu on the table. Dixon waived her off as they continued their conversation.

"I'm just not sure what I'm going to do," Dixon said. "This isn't easy for me or my family. They know I want to play a long way from here, which has been difficult for them to take. It's just a lot to handle right now, especially without Tre'vell. I'm not in a place where I feel like I can make a decision. I've gotta think about this some more."

"Well, take your time—just not too much time, OK?"

Dixon nodded again, pausing a moment before speaking.

"All I know is that I won't be going to Bryant, not after what they did to Tre'vell," Dixon said.

Sanders sat up and leaned in as he spoke in a hushed voice. "What are you talkin' about? What did they do to Tre'vell?"

"They killed him, that's what they did."

"*They* killed him? I thought you said the sheriff isn't sure who did this? Who's *they*?"

"You're right—I said the *sheriff* isn't sure who did it. But *I* am."

"Do you think someone connected to Bryant did this?"

Dixon nodded. "It makes me sick to my stomach," Dixon said. "None of this would've ever happened if I would've just kept my mouth shut."

"What are you talkin' about?"

"I don't know. I've already said too much. I've gotta go."

Dixon got up and darted out the door.

Sanders watched the star recruit disappear as his mind whirred. *Dixon thinks someone from Bryant University killed his friend?*

Sanders fished his cell phone out of his pocket and began searching for Coach Raymond's number. In less than three seconds, his phone was ringing.

"Tell me the good news," Raymond said as he answered. "Is Dixon going to join us next year?"

"Not sure about that yet, Coach," Sanders said. "But there's one thing Dixon is sure of."

"Oh, what's that?"

"That someone murdered Tre'vell Baker—and he thinks he knows who did it."

CHAPTER 4

FRANK JOHNSON LOOKED UP from his newspaper and watched Hugh Sanders exit Lagniappe Café. Properly positioned, the paper hid Johnson's presence well enough that neither Dixon nor Sanders noticed him. It was a trick he learned from several spies after getting burned in a corporate espionage scandal.

Johnson folded the paper and began nursing his tepid coffee. He motioned to the waitress to come over and top off his drink. He added a shot of cream before he processed the conversation he just overheard.

"Having a good day, Mr. Johnson?" the waitress asked.

"I'm alive—and Alabama lost yesterday and Bryant didn't. I don't have much to complain about," he said.

While developing several innovative software designs for a private tech company in Hunstville, Johnson nearly quit after one of his ideas was stolen. A mole inside the company ratted out the secret behind one of Johnson's groundbreaking projects and helped a rival company secure the patent first. It cost Johnson a small fortune in stock options and a promotion. Following the incident, he took extra precautions to ensure that his designs were hidden and secure. He worked on a computer that wasn't connected to the Internet, making it nearly impossible to hack. His state-of-the-art home security system presented a formidable challenge to any thief hoping to steal his computer. To test the system, he hired three of the most widely regarded corporate thieves to break into his own home. They all failed. He resumed developing with confidence that his secrets would remain safe.

While a pivotal event in his professional life, it was also the same event that spurred Johnson's hatred for all things Alabama. Though he was never prosecuted for his crime due to lack of evidence, the mole, Harry Williams, was the most obnoxious Alabama fan on the planet—at least he was in Johnson's world. The rumor was that Harry sold the information to a tech firm run by an Alabama graduate in exchange for lifetime box seats at Bryant-Denny Stadium. Johnson had never engaged much in the tussle between Alabama and Bryant's football fans. Though he'd read shocking stories—stories about Alabama fans poisoning trees used to celebrate wins at a rival school or stories about rival fans killing the grass on Alabama's field—he preferred to stay above the fray. As a graduate of Cal Tech, football had no impact on his college experience and he liked it that way. College was about getting an education. But his view changed after Harry stole what was most precious to him. Johnson decided to do his part in stealing what Alabama fans treasured most: winning.

Without much of an idea of where to start, Johnson joined the Bryant University booster club. He bought season tickets and found a few friends to tailgate with on Saturdays in the fall. Over several years, he went from a guy who didn't much like football to a guy who painted his face black and gold for every game. Behind software development, Bryant University football had become his passion.

The longer Johnson lived in Alabama, the more he transformed from a techie nerd from California to a techie nerd who fell in love with all things related to the South. His tailgating friends—none of whom held jobs that required college degrees—introduced him to fishing and hunting. It wasn't long before Johnson was driving a truck with the windows rolled down and singing "Sweet Home Alabama" without any inhibitions. It truly felt like home.

While Johnson transformed outside the office, he transformed inside it, too. He went from being one of the brightest developers at the firm to the top developer. His stock options bonuses and patent royalties turned him into a multimillionaire. With the capital he acquired, he founded his own software development company. He tripled his money before selling controlling interest in the firm so he could spend more time doing what he'd grown to love: fishing, hunting, and following Bryant University football. And although he enjoyed shooting an eight-point buck and snagging a six-pound bass, nothing gave him more joy than when Bryant defeated Alabama. He pictured a drunk Harry Williams sitting on the tailgate of a pickup truck as he wiped away his tears. It made Johnson smile.

These days, Johnson still tailgated with the same crew, but they all sat in his luxury box. His large donations to the athletic program over time eventually earned him a sit-down meeting with Bryant head coach Gerald Gardner. And before long, Johnson agreed to assist coaches on Gardner's staff whenever they needed a little help with a potential recruit.

From January to June, he lived in his home in Saint-Parran, where he enjoyed daily fishing trips. He returned to Huntsville only for brief business meetings. All the locals in

Saint-Parran knew him, though he toned down his passion for Bryant University football. This was Louisiana State football country and it was always best to respect that. But it was November and Bryant requested Johnson's services in Saint-Parran.

A week ago, Johnson had received a call that a pair of five-star recruits from Saint-Parran decided to renege on their commitment to play for Bryant. He had spent plenty of time talking with both Tre'vell Baker and Dominique Dixon. He didn't think anything could sway them from attending Bryant. But something happened on their visit to the school that changed their minds, an unusual turn of events. If anything, recruits came back from an official visit more committed to the school than ever before. But not Baker and Dixon. And Gardner asked Johnson to find out why.

Johnson had only been in Saint-Parran a few days before he learned of the tragic news of Baker's death. Shot right in front of his little brother. In days past, Johnson would've railed about such senseless violence in the South, all over the stupid game of football, no less. But that was before he understood its place and importance in the culture. Nothing shocked him any more, nor would anything make him climb atop a soapbox and chastise anyone for misplaced passions. This was his way of life now, too.

***

Johnson eased his truck along the dirt road that snaked toward Dominique Dixon's house. The Dixons didn't live on the water, but it was close enough. Johnson could hear the faint slapping of the water against the cypress tree roots as he climbed out of his truck and headed for the front door.

Before Johnson even had a chance to knock, Dixon opened the door and stared at him through the weathered screen door.

"What are you doing here?" Dixon asked.

"I wanted to stop by and see how you were doing," Johnson responded. "I heard about Tre'vell and just wanted say how sorry I was and find out if there was anything I could do for you."

Dixon slipped out the screen door and shuffled over to the front porch swing that creaked loudly when he sat in it.

Dixon stared at the ground before finally speaking.

"Is that why you're really here?" Dixon said. "You sure it's not out of some guilt you have or some need to make sure I keep my mouth shut?"

Johnson was taken aback by the accusations. "What do I have to feel guilty about? And what would you need to keep your mouth shut about?"

"I think you know more than you're letting on, Mr. Johnson." Dixon paused a moment as he looked Johnson up and down. "I think you're a snake. And you know what we do to snakes around here?"

Johnson didn't answer the question, nor did he feel like Dixon really wanted one.

"Look, I don't know what you're talking about," Johnson said. "All I know is that something happened on your visit to Bryant that made you change your mind. And I want to know what we can do to change it back."

"Bring back Tre'vell. That'll change it."

Johnson knew there was no worthwhile response to Dixon's request. It was best to remain silent and let the kid vent.

Dixon stared out into the distance before returning his gaze back toward Johnson.

"You did this," Dixon said. "I know you did."

"Did what? Are you suggesting what I think you're suggesting?"

"Don't play dumb with me."

"I'm not playing dumb. I'd just like to know what you're talking about. Like I said before, I'm just here to see what I can do."

"You can't do anything now. It's too late. I should've never listened to you in the first place. Just another rich old man making your way down here to take advantage of us. You don't care about me—you just care about winnin' football games and drinkin' with your friends. But this is my life we're talking about here, and I'll be damned if I'm gonna let you screw it up any more than you already have."

Dixon's voice rose so much as he spoke that it drew his father outside. Mr. Dixon stumbled through the front door and onto the porch.

"H-h-heeeey. Is this man messsin' wit you?" Mr. Dixon asked his son while pointing at Johnson.

Dixon looked down and shook his head.

"It's okay, Pop. I can handle this."

Mr. Dixon shoved his forefinger into Johnson's chest. "Youuuu better leave mah boy alone, ya hear?" He didn't wait for answer before disappearing back inside.

Johnson seized the moment.

"Dominique, your life is only going to get better from here on out. Your destiny is greater than a job you hate that helps you barely survive and leaves you drunk on the weekend. I want to help you achieve greatness. Why is that so hard for you to accept? This isn't about me. This is about you and what I can do to help you succeed in life."

This wasn't the first time Johnson dug deep and pulled

out an inspirational speech. It was utter nonsense that he sold with fervor. Dixon had just about pegged him. Johnson did care about winning football games, though it was more about beating Alabama than anything else. And if the rumors were true that Alabama was Dixon's preferred school, Johnson was going to fight like hell to make sure that never happened.

Dixon stared at the ground in silence.

Johnson patted Dixon on the back before wrapping up his pitch.

"You're good enough to have it all one day, Dominique. But you're also good enough to have anything you want right now. You just say the word, okay?"

Dixon nodded as he remained transfixed on the ground.

Johnson returned to his truck and began heading back toward town. His objective seemed simple enough: get Johnson to recommit to Bryant. But achieving such a goal seemed like a formidable task in the wake of his conversation. Despite his smooth speech, Johnson knew Dixon was angry over what happened to Baker. And he couldn't blame the kid either.

But something had happened on Baker and Dixon's visit to Bryant. Nobody knew what it was—at least if they did, they weren't telling him about it. If he had any hope of success, he needed to know what it was that happened. He needed to know why Tre'vell Baker was dead—and he needed to know why Dixon thought he had something to do with it.

CHAPTER 5

ON MONDAY MORNING, CAL TRUDGED through security at Atlanta Hartsfield-Jackson International Airport. He wondered how the busiest airport in the world could be so inept at screening so many passengers. It was a nightmare as usual. Long lines full of grumpy business travelers who had yet to ingest the necessary level of caffeine to ease the pain of waiting to be either frisked, wanded or X-rayed. Cal just wanted to be on his plane for New Orleans and grab a few extra minutes of sleep.

Once the TSA agents determined Cal posed no imminent threat to the airplane, he gathered his belongings and headed toward his terminal.

As he neared his departure gate, Cal stopped at a small bookstore. All the latest bestsellers filled a small shelf. At the bottom of the list, he noticed a title that interested him: "MUSCLE: How the NFL went from 0 to 100 on the back of performance enhancing drugs." Then he saw the author's name—Barry Anderson. The book held the eighth position on *The New York Times'* bestseller list.

The bestseller list? If Barry can do this, so can I.

Cal plunked a twenty-dollar bill on the counter to buy the book. He needed to know how this was done if he was going to land that big contract Mike Nicholson told him was there for the taking if this mystery in the bayou unfolded the way he was told it would.

***

When Cal exited the New Orleans airport and headed toward the transportation area, he saw his name scribbled on a tattered cardboard sign: "Cal Murphy." Holding the sign was a chubby man who appeared to be in his 40s and had a distinct disdain for grooming. His soiled Remington cap tried to hide the scraggly salt and pepper hair curling beneath it. He wore a pair of dirty jeans with boots and a brown down vest atop a red short-sleeve t-shirt.

"Are you Cal Murphy?" the man asked as he walked slowly toward Cal.

Cal nodded. When his editor suggested he get a guide, Cal scoffed. But then he relented, concluding that it might be a good idea to have a local on his side. Now, Cal was wondering why he didn't protest more and trust his first instinct.

"Pleased to meet you, Mr. Murphy," the man said as he offered his hand. "My name is Phil Potter and I'm supposed to take you to Saint-Parran today."

Cal shook Potter's hand and acted as polite as possible. This was Cal's first time in Louisiana—and it wasn't at all what he expected. Quite frankly, he wasn't sure what he expected. Drunken revelers during Mardi Gras, crazy Cajuns on a reality TV show, and despondent homeowners during Hurricane Katrina were the images conjured up in his mind when anyone mentioned this unique state. But it was evident that this was a different kind of place, the kind of place that made Cal feel like a foreigner.

Potter led Cal to his truck and threw his carry-on luggage into the bed. He covered it with a tarp that buttoned down along the edges of the truck bed.

"That ain't goin' nowhere," Potter said as he smiled at Cal before slapping the side of the truck and unlocking the doors.

Cal opened the door and used the handle to propel himself onto the running board and into the truck that appeared to be jacked at least a couple of feet in the air. He searched awkwardly for the seatbelt before wrangling it and securing it. The smell of tobacco emanated through the vehicle. Cal stared at the handful of empty tobacco tins that littered the floorboard.

"Sorry about the mess," Potter said as the engine roared to life.

Cal gave him a friendly nod and smiled. *If he was that sorry, he would've cleaned it out before he picked me up.*

"First time in Louisiana?" Potter asked, trying to engage Cal in a conversation.

"Yes, it is."

"Well, I hope you enjoy your time here. It's a heckuva place. I've lived here a long time and wouldn't want to live anywhere else."

"Where else have you lived?" Cal asked.

"Just Louisiana. But I know it's the greatest place to live on earth. More fishin' and huntin' than you can shake a stick at."

"Sounds like a great place … if you like that sort of thing."

Potter paid the parking attendant and steered his truck toward the Interstate.

"You hunt and fish much, Mr. Murphy?"

"Please, call me Cal."

"Okay, Cal it is. Do you hunt and fish much, Cal?"

"Not very often. I used to do some hunting and fishing when I was a kid but I haven't had much time for it lately."

"Work keep ya busy?"

"You could say that?"

"So, you comin' to Saint-Parran to reconnect with your childhood?"

"No, actually, I'm coming here on business."

"Business? What kind of business does anyone have in Saint-Parran other than fishin' and huntin'?"

Cal paused before answering. He'd just met Potter and wasn't sure how much information to divulge.

"I'm a sports writer and I'm writing a story on some big-time college football recruits." It was a safe response.

"Well, that's good to know. I assume you want to talk to Dominique Dixon then."

"That's what I'd like to do. Do you know him?"

"We're goin' to Saint-Parran, Cal, not the boomin' metropolis of Atlanta. I know everybody that lives within twenty miles of Lagniappe Café."

"Is that in the center of town?"

Potter nodded. "And the best coffee in Louisiana."

Potter turned west onto Highway 90 as the signs of big city life began to disappear in the rearview mirror.

For the next hour and a half the scenery shifted from metropolitan skyline to swampland, as Cal gathered a healthy background of Saint-Parran from his well-versed chauffeur. For starters, most residents in the area believed the city was cursed when it was founded by a handful of runaway slaves a few years before slavery was abolished. A witch doctor cast a spell on the place when he learned his cousin had escaped there and refused to take him along. Since the city was founded, at least one person had been killed by either an alligator or a black bear every year. Potter said the people of Saint-Parran never much minded the curse since the people who usually ended up dead were hunters and fishermen who "weren't usin' their noggins." It was rare for Saint-Parran to go this late into the year without such a death, though Potter said many of the townspeople believed Tre'vell Baker's mysterious death would fill that spot if no one else ended up dead in the swamp due to a wildlife attack.

Potter also went on to explain how the town's economy was fed primarily through adventurous outdoorsmen and marine biologists. The bayou's unique ecology made for both a fertile laboratory and a diverse place to fish and hunt. Peppe's Outfitters employed the most guides followed by Geaux For It Outfitters and Billy's Bayou Adventures, the latter of which employed Potter. Cal hadn't seen a single picture of Billy's Bayou Adventures, but he didn't have to use much imagination after meeting his chauffeur.

As they turned south onto Highway 1 and slipped deeper into the bayou, Potter divulged a few things that were more important to Cal's potential story. For starters, Saint-Parran was the part-time home to quite a few wealthy boosters from a number of major colleges in the south, including Alabama, Bryant University, Louisiana State, Ole Miss, Mississippi State, Arkansas, and Tennessee. However, none of the worthy student athletes ever went anywhere but Louisiana State, thanks to Wesley Tucker. Tucker owned a regional bank that had branches all along the coastal areas of Louisiana, Mississippi and Alabama. He used his influence and money to steer recruits in the area to Baton Rouge to play for Louisiana State.

According to Potter, Randall Blackledge, owner of

Geaux For It Outfitters, was languishing near bankruptcy until his son Bobby became one of the most sought-after quarterbacks in the southeast. Louisiana State was eager to attract Bobby since the best quarterback they had was an accused rapist that had been kicked out of Tennessee and couldn't throw a pass longer than forty yards. In a development that shocked recruiting analysts, Bobby spurned Alabama, Florida, and Texas for Louisiana State. In a development that wasn't as shocking, Geaux For It Outfitters moved from near bankruptcy to rival Peppe's in grandeur and staffing almost overnight. The story went that Tucker would forgive Blackledge's debt if he nurtured his son in the direction of Louisiana State. The Florida coaches pitched a hissy fit and reported the allegations to the NCAA, but no wrongdoing was ever proven.

"That Wesley Tucker always covers his tracks," Potter said. "It's hard to find dirt in the swamp."

Potter told several more tales of recruiting coups for Louisiana State, all at the hands of Wesley Tucker. He retold these stories with pride, hinting that he felt such actions were justified if it meant getting those hometown boys to play for his team.

"So are you a big Louisiana State fan?" Cal asked.

"We say LSU down here," Potter corrected. "Now, I don't drive to Baton Rouge every Saturday in the fall to watch the games, if that's what you mean. I work on the weekends. But I always bring a radio to listen to the games while we're out on the water. It passes the time, especially when the fish ain't bitin'."

They rode along in silence for a few minutes before Cal went on a little fishing expedition of his own.

"So what do you know about these two kids, Baker and

Dixon?" Cal asked.

"What do you mean?"

"I mean, were they good kids?"

"All the kids around here are good."

"I mean, were they into anything that you know of?"

"Like what?"

"Drugs? Gangs? Illegal activities?"

"Well, Cal, there ain't none of that to get into around Saint-Parran. It's fishin' and huntin' and football. And from what I know of those kids seeing them around town, ain't nothing but model citizens."

"Good to know."

Potter wasn't done.

"That's what made Tre'vell's death so shockin'. Nobody would hurt that kid if they knew him. He was a saint, always helpin' people. His mama worked her tail off to support those four boys and Tre'vell always did what he could to help her. He would've been a star in the NFL, no doubt in my mind. He coulda rescued his whole family out of the poor house."

"What about Dominique?"

"He's a good kid, too. Not quite as helpful as Tre'vell, but good all the same." Potter paused for a moment before continuing. "It's just a shame what happened, a plumb shame."

Just as Potter looked like he might cry, his countenance suddenly changed. He kept both hands on the steering wheel but gestured with his right index finger toward the sign along the side of the road.

"Welcome to Saint-Parran, Cal," he said. "Home of the best fishin' and huntin' in all of Louisiana."

"And coffee, too," Cal added.

"And coffee, too," Potter said. "Nothin' gets by you does it?"

Cal smiled. Nothing better get by him if he wanted to uncover the truth behind Tre'vell Baker's death. Cal was on high alert from the minute he stepped off the plane two hours before.

"So, where you wanna go?" Potter asked. "I'm yours for the whole week. Just say the word and I'll take you wherever you wanna go. Wanna get settled in first?"

Cal shook his head. "There'll be plenty of time for that later," he said. "Why don't you take me to see the sheriff?"

"You've been in town two minutes and you want to see Sheriff Mouton?" Potter asked incredulously. "You don't mess around, do you?"

"No, I don't."

"Well, hold on. You ain't ever met a sheriff like Sheriff Mouton."

CHAPTER 6

THE SHERIFF'S OFFICE for Toulon Parish lacked attention to detail from top to bottom. The two windows flanking the front door allowed both wind and sunlight in, yet not too much of either one. Cal thought he might fall through the floor as the boards beneath him squeaked with the weight of each step. The calendar tacked to the wall behind the receptionist was two years behind, though Cal wasn't sure if he was stepping into a law enforcement office or a time warp.

If they handle their cases like they handle their upkeep, no wonder they haven't arrested anyone for Baker's murder.

Potter, who led Cal into the sheriff's office, wasted no time in making small talk with Bernice Grant, the bespectacled aging receptionist. For what Potter lacked in professional appearance, he made up for it with surprising aplomb. He looked comfortable on his own turf. The conversation meandered from the weather to Louisiana State football to a recipe for gator tail soup. This went on for several minutes before Potter introduced Cal to Bernice and stated the purpose of their visit.

"Is Sheriff Mouton around?" Potter asked.

"Are you kiddin' me? Monday mornings are all about

paperwork around here," Bernice said as she shuffled papers on her desk. "And when it comes to paperwork, Sheriff Mouton is about as useful as an ashtray on a motorcycle."

Cal snickered at Bernice's wisecrack but realized she wasn't laughing—or even smiling.

"So, what brings you down to our parts, Mr. Big City Reporter?" Bernice asked.

"I'm working on a story about Tre'vell Baker's death," he said.

"Oh, what a shame that is. That boy could've been a star in the NFL one day. Just tragic."

Cal slipped his notepad out, hoping to get some background worthy fodder from the sassy secretary. "Did you know Tre'vell?"

"Know Tre'vell? Look, Metro Man, I know everybody in this town, just like Potter here. We're like a family. It's a little different than your big city life."

Cal resisted the urge to match her sardonic wit. "So, what can you tell me about him?"

"He was a heckuva kid with a heart of gold. Is that what you're looking for?" Bernice said. She yanked open a filing cabinet and shoved some papers into it without hesitating. "I mean, he was classy, just like his mama. You'd be proud to have a son like him one day."

Cal paused for a moment as Bernice's last comment sank in. He would've been proud to have *any* son at this point in his life, part of the reason for his trip here in the first place. Yet he couldn't let such thoughts distract him. "Did Tre'vell have any enemies?"

Bernice stopped her busy work, something Cal figured was unnecessary and designed to impress him. She looked up at him over the top of her glasses. "Enemies? In Saint-Parran?

Son, you've got a lot to learn about this place. We all need each other around here. We might have a few family spats here and there, but the residents who live here year-round would never do something like this to one another—I don't care if they are drunk as a skunk sliding off their stool at Wahoo's Watering Hole. People don't kill each other around here."

Cal took note of Bernice's careful word usage. "What about residents that don't live here year-round?"

Bernice threw her hands up in the air as she answered. "Oh, now, I can't vouch for them. Who knows what they'd do? We sure do appreciate their money, but not their company. Most of 'em are harmless, enjoyin' their dwindlin' days here on earth. But there are a few jokers I wouldn't invite to my Aunt Lettie's Christmas brunch, if you know what I mean." She gave him a little wink.

Cal was pretty sure he knew what she meant. He gave her a little wink back. "I appreciate your help, Miss Grant."

"Please, call me Bernice," she shot back. "You let me know if I can help you with anything else or if you want to know where the best place to get a sweet tea is in this town."

"Wouldn't that be Lagniappe Café?" Cal asked as he looked back at Potter, who remained quiet throughout their conversation.

"You're either a quick learner or Phil here's already told you that Lagniappe Café is the only restaurant in town."

Cal nodded and smiled. "I do have one more question for you."

"Shoot, honey."

"Where can we find Sheriff Mouton?"

"You won't find him around here, but ole Phil can take you to him. He's most likely shootin' up a few targets out at Willie's old place."

Cal looked at Potter as if to ask if he knew where this location was.

Potter nodded. "I can take you there. Let's go."

Cal smiled and thanked Bernice again for her help.

After they exited the office, Potter chuckled to himself as he unlocked his truck.

"What are you laughing about?" Cal asked as he pulled himself aboard.

"That Bernice," he said as he fired up the engine. "She's a character now. But I think she warmed up to you right nice."

"I wasn't sure at first. I thought she was going to bite my head off."

Potter eased the truck on the road and glanced over at Cal. "She still might."

***

Fifteen minutes later, Potter wheeled his truck onto a piece of property that looked more abandoned than Cal imagined. Rotten fence posts struggled to hold strands of rusty barbed wire. A dirt driveway riddled with potholes led them to a house that looked like it might not survive the next strong breeze. With an auburn-colored tin roof leaning into the interior of the house, the structure looked more like a scrap heap.

"Welcome to Willie Hebert's old farm," Potter announced. He slowed down as they neared the house.

"Somebody lives here?" Cal asked.

"Shoot, no. Somebody *lived* here. The late great Mr. Willie Hebert."

"And what happened to Willie?"

"Gator got him. He already had one bum leg from an

alligator attack as a kid. Guess it came back to finish the job."

"He died from an alligator bite?"

"I wouldn't call it a bite—more like a maulin'. Nobody knows for sure how long his body was sittin' out in the sun. Or if he looked so bad because of the alligator or the other wild critters that munched on him after he was dead. Either way, ole Willie's funeral was a closed casket service."

"I didn't think alligators were all that dangerous."

"Stick around—and watch yer back. You'll find out soon enough just how dangerous they are."

Potter parked and exited the vehicle with Cal in tow. The eerie silence soon vanished amidst an eruption of gunshots. Cal jumped and ducked, fearing someone was shooting at him. Potter chuckled before grabbing him by the arm.

"Get up, city slicker," Potter said. "Ain't you ever heard gunshots before?"

"Plenty of times," Cal answered. "And most of the time they were shooting at me."

"I guess maybe big city life and the bayou ain't so different after all."

Cal resisted the urge to educate Potter on his dangerous real world exploits. If Potter was half the guide he claimed to be, it might be best if he believed Cal was a weakling who needed his protection.

They rounded the corner of the dilapidated house to find two uniformed law enforcement officers shooting rifles at targets several hundred feet away. A young, puny officer saw Potter and Cal approaching and tapped the larger man on the shoulder, a man Cal assumed was Sheriff Mouton. The man didn't move, keeping dead aim on the target until he fired off a shot.

"Well?" Sheriff Mouton asked his deputy.

The deputy scrambled to put his binoculars up to his eyes and report his findings on the shot. "Just a little to the left of the bulls eye."

"Dang thing still ain't sighted in right. Here, fix it, Milton," Sheriff Mouton said as he handed the gun to his deputy. Then he spun around to talk to his guests.

"Well, Potter, to what do we owe this visit—and who's the carpetbagger you got with ya?" Sheriff Mouton said as he guffawed.

"Sheriff, this here is Cal Murphy, a reporter from Atlanta who is writin' a story on a couple of our star athletes."

Cal nodded and smiled. "Pleased to meet you, Sheriff Mouton."

"The pleasure will be all yours, I'm sure," Sheriff Mouton shot back. "Look, I don't know what you think you're doing down here, but this is my parish and I don't really like people stickin' their noses where they don't belong. I'm sure you're here about Tre'vell and Dominique."

"Just writing about Dominique for now."

"I doubt that. Don't you be tryin' to solve Tre'vell's murder on your own. The swamp ain't a friendly place to outsiders."

"I understand, Sheriff," Cal answered. "I'm not trying to do your job for you. I'm just here to write a story about Dominique and I'm sure some of that story will include how the community is handling Tre'vell's loss."

"You sure better not be here to find out how I'm handlin' my investigation into Tre'vell's death. Cause I'll ride you hard and put you up wet. You'll wish you never came down here, ya hear?"

"Loud and clear, Sheriff." This wasn't the first time someone in law enforcement tried to intimidate Cal. He remained resolute in his purpose for visiting Sheriff Mouton.

Sheriff Mouton then whipped his pistol out of his holster and riddled with holes another target about 20 yards away. He then jammed the gun back into the holster and spun around to look at Cal.

"Impressive," Cal said without a hint of patronage. "So, I had a few questions for you, if that's all right."

"Shoot," Sheriff Mouton said.

Cal pulled out his notepad and recorder before proceeding. "Do you have any suspects in Tre'vell's death?"

"Not yet, but we're looking into a few leads."

"What kind of leads?" Cal asked.

"Good ones, I hope. But I won't know until I investigate a little further."

"Any leads that might give you a clue as to a motive?"

"This is off the record cause I don't want this gettin' out," Sheriff Mouton said and waited until Cal stopped writing. "Now, we found a crumpled up note in Tre'vell's bag that said, 'Don't make the biggest mistake of your life.' Now, I don't know if it's from a girl or his mama or some punk who was mad about where he was goin' to school. But that's about all I've got to go on at the moment when it comes to determin' motive."

Cal scribbled down a few notes then flipped a few pages before asking another question.

"Did you know of anyone who would want to hurt Tre'vell? From all accounts I've heard, he was a pretty good kid."

"Who you been talkin' to? His mama?"

Cal bristled at the way Sheriff Mouton dismissed him. He wasn't one to lie down for a pompous lawman, even if he was in a world he didn't quite understand.

"Excuse me?" Cal retorted with a twinge of disdain.

"Listen, if there's one thing I've learned as sheriff of Toulon Parish it's that nobody's ever innocent. Victim or accused criminal—they've all got somethin' hidden deep that they don't want anybody to see. Now, it's my job to find out what they've done to suffer such a sudden demise. You find that out, you can just about find out every time who done it. Just keep hangin' around me, son, and you might just yet become a good reporter."

Cal seethed as he flipped his notebook shut and politely thanked Sheriff Mouton for his time. Then he turned to walk away.

"Where you goin' so fast, son? Don't you know Potter's gotta get a round off first?" Sheriff Mouton asked.

Sheriff Mouton and his deputy laughed as Potter sneered.

"I don't have to prove anything to you, Sheriff," Potter said. "You know I'm a good shot."

"Yep, you're such a good shot that you don't lead any more huntin' expeditions. I'm sure you forgot to inform your companion about that fact."

More laughing ensued. Cal watched as Potter grew enraged.

"Gimme that," Potter said as he snatched the rifle out of the deputy's hands.

Potter lay on his stomach and steadied the gun. He stared through the scope for several seconds before Sheriff Mouton distracted him.

"Don't forget that we're aimin' for the target and not some random tree out there."

Potter looked up and glared at the sheriff. He then returned his focus to the scope and aimed the gun. A crack ripped through the swamp, sending a flock of birds skyward.

After a few seconds, the deputy started laughing.

"What is it, Milton?" Sheriff Mouton asked.

"Potter better look out. There's an angry tree out there that's going to come after him," the deputy said.

Potter bristled. "That gun ain't sighted in right."

"No, it ain't," Sheriff Mouton said. "But I doubt that would've made much difference to a guy who couldn't hit the ocean standing on the beach."

"Oh, you're full of good one-liners today," Potter said.

"I always am."

Despite the fact that Cal found the situation humorous, he resisted the urge to laugh at his guide. The week was just beginning.

"Now, watch yourself with this 'un," Sheriff Mouton said to Cal as he pointed at Potter. "If you get yourself in a fix, call us. If Potter starts shootin', you might not make it back to Atlanta in one piece, but that'd only be if he got lucky and hit you by mistake. If he's aimin' at you, you got nothin' to worry about."

Cal smiled, nodded and thanked the sheriff again before he turned and walked with Potter toward the truck. Another round of gunshots echoed throughout the surrounding woods.

"A lot of help he was," Cal groused once he climbed into the truck and shut the door.

"Aww, that's just Sheriff Mouton," Potter said. "You get used to it after a while. He wasn't elected cause he's the friendliest son of a gun around here, but he almost always finds his man."

"Almost always?" Cal asked.

"He's not perfect, if you ask me. He's a little arrogant

and that's his downfall sometimes."

"Well, who do you think would've written a note like that to Tre'vell?"

"I ain't gotta clue. The swamp's got as many crazies as it does critters."

CHAPTER 7

DOMINIQUE DIXON KEPT his standing appointment at the Texaco convenience store immediately after school. He and Tre'vell used to grab a couple of quarts of Gatorade and energy bars before football practice. Alone on this excursion for the first time, Dixon struggled to see through bleary eyes as he walked around the store. He grabbed double of everything he needed as he intended to set up a makeshift shrine at practice.

Dixon refused to make eye contact with Tammy, the clerk who worked the afternoon shift. She told him she was sorry to hear about Tre'vell. Dixon nodded, handed her exact change and stumbled outside. He wiped away a tear with his sleeve and then got into his car. That's when Dixon lost it. He'd briefly cried when he first heard the news, but now reality weighed upon him. Tre'vell was gone, and he wasn't ever coming back.

He rolled the window down on his Civic and turned the ignition key as it sputtered to life. Parked along the side of the convenience store, Dixon didn't move. It wasn't fair, he thought. Tre'vell Baker was one of the good guys, the kind of kid who'd do anything for you, even if it wasn't convenient for him. Yet it was his good heart that put him on the losing end of a bullet fired by some mystery person for who knows what. None of it made sense. Tre'vell was friends with everybody. How could anyone hurt such a kid?

Dixon snapped back to reality when a silver Range Rover parked right next to him. It was Frank Johnson. Dixon eyed Johnson as he rounded his vehicle and approached him. Johnson put his hands on the door and stooped down to eye level with Dixon.

"Hi, Dominique."

Dixon wasn't in the mood. He didn't want to talk recruiting with Bryant University's biggest booster in the Louisiana bayou. He figured a cold response might get rid of him. "Sorry to hear about your loss."

"My loss? What are you talking about?"

"That whippin' LSU put on your boys two weeks ago."

Johnson grunted and muttered something that sounded to Dixon something like "those crooked bayou refs," but he couldn't be sure.

"Look, I know you're still grieving. Heck, we all are. Tre'vell was a great kid and I was hoping to see both of you join the Bryant family. But you've still got some big decisions to make. And I think you've got an offer you can't easily dismiss."

"I don't really want to talk about it right now, Mr. Johnson."

"Fair enough. But just remember that you aren't going to get a deal like you're getting with Bryant anywhere else."

Dixon snickered but said nothing.

"Oh, has Alabama finally decided to get serious about you?"

Dixon shook his head and said nothing.

Johnson continued his pitch. "Cause if they are, I might be able to up the ante, so to speak."

Dixon stared straight ahead, refusing to speak.

"All right, suit yourself. You know where to find me."

With that, Johnson turned and walked away. However, he paused for a moment and dropped a plastic card on the ground. He looked at it for a moment and then walked away.

"Mr. Johnson, you dropped something," Dixon said.

Johnson looked back at Dixon. "I didn't drop anything." He grinned and then climbed back into his Range Rover before driving away.

Dixon shook his head and looked up to see Saint-Parran quarterback D.J. Garnett staring at him.

"What was that all about?" Garnett asked Dixon as he approached his car.

Dixon shook his head. "Crazy old man won't leave me alone."

"Is that the Bryant guy?" Garnett asked.

Dixon nodded.

Garnett looked at the ground at the plastic card. "Did you drop this?" He handed the card to Dixon.

"I didn't, but I'll take it."

"Oh, one of those 'gifts' you're not supposed to get?" Garnett asked.

"Yeah, definitely not supposed to get those. But if that old man still thinks I might go to Bryant, I might milk him dry."

"He's definitely got a sweet ride." Garnett then looked at Dixon's beat-up Civic. "Maybe you can get him to get you a car next time instead of a stupid little gift card."

Garnett flung the card into Dixon's window and left.

Practice started in ten minutes and Coach Holloway didn't tolerate tardiness.

***

A somber mood rested over practice. Dixon was convinced the Saint Parran Tigers were destined for the state championship game with some unlucky team in the Mercedes-Benz Superdome in New Orleans. It was the number one goal written on the chalkboard at the beginning of the season. And a few short days ago, it seemed not only possible but probable. The Tigers mauled their opponents all season long, including perennial powerhouse Haynesville. But Baker was the main reason why. Without Baker, Dixon felt like destiny had abandoned them.

Halfway through practice, head coach Hal Holloway ceased the current drill and ordered everyone to the center of the field.

"I know every one of you guys is hurtin' right now," Holloway began. "We've all lost a friend and dang good player in Tre'vell. But if we really want to honor his memory, we can't sit around here mopin' and goin' through the motions. Life goes on. And if Tre'vell could speak to us today, he'd tell us to go out there and win this thing for him. There'll be plenty of time to cry and think about our friend. But we've still got a football game Friday night and I want us to make him proud. He's going to be lookin' down on us and rootin' hard. Let's not disappoint him, OK?"

The players responded with a half-hearted "OK, coach." Then Dixon stood up.

"Tre'vell and I were best friends, and I'm hurtin', too," Dixon said. "We're all hurtin'. But nothin' is going to make the pain go away. Tre'vell was the best friend and teammate we could ever ask for."

Dixon paused and pointed toward the Gatorade and

power bar sitting on one of the benches along the sideline.

"I don't want to forget the sacrifices that Tre'vell made for this team each and every day," he said as he looked at the small memorial. "He loved each and every one of us. And I want to dedicate this week's game and the rest of the season to him. Let's write his number on our shoes, our gloves, our pads, our helmets. But most importantly, let's write his memory on our hearts. Who's with me?"

The players' responses were more animated than after Coach Holloway's speech. But it wasn't enough for Dixon.

"I said, 'Who's with me?'" he barked.

The entire team in unison responded with a roar.

Dixon looked over at Coach Holloway and winked. Coach Holloway smiled back. Then Dixon called the entire team into the center and they began a series of chants.

Dixon made sure nobody would forget Tre'vell Baker any time soon.

CHAPTER 8

POTTER TURNED THE CORNER past the Texaco gas station and onto the road leading to Saint-Parran's football stadium.

"Coach Holloway will still have the boys out working hard," Potter said. "They barely scraped by a terrible team in their final regular season game. I'll bet they'll be running bleachers by the time we get there."

Once Potter parked the truck, he and Cal got out and strolled toward the stadium.

Even before Cal could fully take in the scene, he knew Potter was right. Through the slats in the bleachers, Cal could see a mass of legs pumping up and down the steps.

"I'll be danged," Potter mumbled. "Holloway is one of the most predictable coaches on the planet. I'd be willing to bet it was his fault the game was so close and not the kids'."

Cal nodded and plodded toward the stadium.

With gold letters "Tiger Stadium" etched on the exterior of the stadium's black press box, the venue reminded Cal of the rest of Saint-Parrain: plain and simple. A six-foot high chain link fence surrounded the stadium. The main gate remained open and used only a weathered eight-foot table as a ticket hub. Covering games in everything from eight-man high school football fields without lights to NFL stadiums, Cal estimated the stadium seated a little over two thousand fans. About two thousand on the home side and a couple hundred in the visitors' section. A press box, one in desperate need of a paint job, decked the top of the home side stands with room for no more than two-dozen people.

When Cal turned his attention to the field, he spotted Coach Holloway immediately, based on Potter's description. A hefty man who loved two things: chewing tobacco and coaching football. Holloway's most distinguishing characteristic was his raspy voice that echoed through the vacant stadium as he barked at the players running up and down the bleacher steps.

"Come on, McGrath! You're lumbering!" Holloway chided one of his players. "You think you're gonna catch a quarterback in the fourth quarter with the game on the line movin' that slow? My grandma could move with her walker faster than you're movin' right now!"

Potter leaned over toward Cal.

"Holloway's right, you know," Potter said. "His grandma used to come to every game until she died a couple of years ago. I saw her run down a young punk who tried to steal her purse at a game once. She wrapped her walker around the kid before he gave her his wallet to stop."

Cal chuckled at Potter's exaggerated tale.

"They even have a play named in her honor. It's called 'Grandma H,' " Potter said. "It's a pick play where one of the receivers blows up a defensive back on a crossin' route. It's just how Grandma H would've wanted it."

If Coach Holloway was half as colorful as Potter's description of Grandma H, Cal figured an interesting interview awaited him.

Cal and Potter stopped at a short chain link fence encircling the playing field. Cal rested on the fence as he watched Coach Holloway in action.

Ten minutes later, practice ended with Coach Holloway imploring his kids to stay focused and out of trouble since they had a big game coming up on Friday night. He mentioned how practice would be delayed an hour on Thursday so everyone could go to Baker's funeral. Dixon led the team in a series of chants before they scattered across the field and toward their vehicles.

Coach Holloway spotted Cal and Potter and ambled toward his two guests.

"Well, who left the gate open?" Coach Holloway asked. He didn't wait for a reply. "When I first saw you two across the field, I thought you were enemy spies and I was ready to come over here and rip you guys a new one."

Cal didn't doubt that Coach Holloway would. The coach waited a moment before he smiled, which eased Cal's mind. Before introductions began, Coach Holloway held out his hand to Cal and squeezed it so tight Cal thought at least three bones in his hands were crushed.

"What's your name, fella? I don't think I've had the pleasure of meetin' you."

"Cal Murphy."

"And what brings you to Saint-Parran, Mr. Cal Murphy?"

Before Cal could answer, Potter butted in.

"This is the reporter I was tellin' you about that I'm going to be takin' around for a few days while he's investigatin' for his story."

Coach Holloway turned toward Cal. "Story about what?"

"Story about Dominique Dixon and Tre'vell Baker's recruitment and the mystery surroundin' Baker's death," Potter said, stealing Cal's chance to speak.

"Well, I'm afraid you're going to be disappointed. His death is as big of a mystery as we've ever had in Toulon Parish. There ain't no good reason anybody would want to kill that kid. He was a gem."

"Mind if I ask you a few questions about him? I'm trying to get a better picture of who he was," Cal said.

"Oh, I don't mind at all." Coach Holloway looked off in the distance as he adjusted the wad of chewing tobacco in his mouth with his tongue. "Go ahead, son. The world ain't standing still."

Flustered by the coach's impatience, Cal flipped through his notes until he came upon his set of questions for the coach.

"How would you describe Tre'vell Baker as a person and as a football player?" Cal asked.

"There was no difference with him. On and off the field, he was a firecracker—full of passion and energy. A natural leader. Always looking out for the best interest of others. I think that's why this team loved him so much."

Cal jotted down some notes before asking his next question.

"Now, did you ever see anything about Tre'vell that would ever give you a reason to be concerned?"

"Concerned about what?"

"Concerned that maybe he was getting into some stuff that he wasn't supposed to?"

"Tre'vell?" Coach Holloway asked. It was as if he didn't believe Cal asked him this question. Cal nodded. "Are you kiddin' me? That kid was pure gold. If he had any flaw, it was in being too good to the people around him."

"What do you mean by that?"

"I mean that Tre'vell would give you the shirt off his back if you asked him. And you knew darn well the kid didn't have another shirt at home. That's just the kind of kid he was. Lord knows how that boy had such a good heart. It certainly didn't come from his absent father."

Cal scribbled down a few more notes.

"Did he say anything to you after his trip to Bryant University with Dominique Dixon?"

"Like what?"

"Like why he was reneging on his verbal commitment to attend school there?"

"Not really. He just said he wasn't as impressed now and wanted to keep his options open." Coach Holloway paused. "Are you implyin' that his death had somethin' to do with him changin' his mind about where he was going to play ball?"

"I'm just asking questions. I don't know anything but I'm trying to get educated."

"Well, I'll tell you all you need to know." Coach Holloway paused, creating a moment of drama in the conversation. "Some coward shot that kid for no good reason. He probably thought he was a deer or a bear and got all trigger happy. But whatever the reason, it won't bring Tre'vell back now. We've all just got to move on and think about how much better our lives are for knowin' him. And I suggest you do the same, Mr. Cal Murphy."

Cal paused from his note taking and looked up. "Do the same?"

"Yeah, just move on. Ain't nothin' good ever comes out of dredgin' the swamp of a person's life."

Cal nodded and thanked the coach for his time. It was clear the interview was over.

CHAPTER 9

ON TUESDAY MORNING, Frank Johnson paced back and forth outside his hangar at the Saint-Parran Airfield. Like most airfields without a tower, the Saint-Parran Airfield consisted of nothing more than a long strip of pavement, a windsock and a few hangars. Instead of a fence, a line of thick trees served as a weak deterrent. On more than one occasion, planes aborted landing due to wildlife moseying across the airstrip. The planes that frequented Saint-Parran the most chose to use waterways for takeoffs and landings, if possible. The local airfield remained reserved almost exclusively for the wealthy migratory hunters.

Johnson stared at his Rolex and tapped the glass. *He should be here by now.* Before Johnson could worry another second, he heard the faint roar of his Gulfstream IV's jet engines. Within minutes, the plane was on the ground and taxiing toward his hangar.

As the engines powered down, Johnson awaited for the door to open and his guest to disembark. Like a star-crossed fan, Johnson approached Bryant University head coach Gerald Gardner as he stepped onto the Louisiana ground.

"It's so good to see you, Coach Gardner," Johnson said. "I trust your flight went smoothly."

Gardner flashed his trademark smile, offering to shake Johnson's hand. "Your crew always treats me like a rock star, Frank. I appreciate that. As always, everything was perfect."

The two began to walk away from the plane and toward Johnson's Range Rover.

"So, bring me up to speed," Gardner said. "What's happening with Dixon? Are we going to lose him?"

Johnson unlocked his vehicle with his key fob and they both climbed in.

"It's hard to say, Coach," Johnson began, "but it's not looking very promising at this point. He's grieving his friend—but he's also greedy. Not sure that we'll be able to offer enough to satisfy him."

"The Lord giveth and taketh away," Gardner said.

Johnson cranked the engine and began heading for the airfield exit.

"Yeah, I'm not sure about all that. For the moment, I think one of our top recruits is just being taken away by those vile imbeciles from Alabama."

"Now, now, Frank. Let's not get all judgmental. Besides, there's another verse I like: 'Vengeance is mine, sayeth the Lord.' "

"That's the kind of verse I like," Johnson said. He smiled and turned onto the major road leading to Saint-Parran. "You still have plenty of work to do, but I think we can still get him."

As they drove through town, Gardner shook his head. "Same ole, Saint-Parran. This place hasn't changed a lick."

Johnson shot a glance toward his passenger. "You've been here before?"

"Yep, long time ago when I was on the coaching staff at Texas. They had a kid down here named Harvey Clarkston who was one of the hardest-hitting linebackers I'd ever seen. He was tougher than a two-dollar steak but he couldn't spell his own name if his life depended on it."

"Did you sign him?"

"Unfortunately not. Mind you, this was back in the days when there was no dead period before signing day. Nowadays, a coach can't have contact with a recruit after Sunday the week before signing day. But back then? Everything was fair game. We used to sequester kids to make sure some other school's coach didn't get to them right before signing day and change their mind. So, anyway, I could've sworn we had Clarkston wrapped up until Miami swooped in right before we got here and hid him away. I staked out his house and thought I saw him leave. By the time I caught up with him in the Piggly Wiggly parking lot, I found out he gave me the slip and signed a letter of intent to play for Miami in the meat department. That coach waved the letter at me as he exited the store. I wanted to punch him in the mouth."

"How'd he do at Miami?"

"He never set foot on the field. It was a plumb shame. Those coaches screwed him up. He should've gone to Texas."

Johnson scratched his face and pondered his next comment.

"Well, Dixon's as sharp as a tack."

"Not if he's thinking about going to Alabama," Gardner quipped. A wry smile spread across his face. He looked at Johnson, who was also smiling.

"I knew there was a good reason we made you the head coach of Bryant."

***

By the time Dominique Dixon arrived home from Tuesday's practice, two guests awaited him. Frank Johnson and Bryant University head coach Gerald Gardner sat on the front porch of his house, sipping sweet tea and trading stories with his mom. Dixon looked at the scene and rolled his eyes. The whole recruiting process felt like a sham to him. Coaches selling him and his parents on the virtues of a good education at their school along with the kind of coaching he needed to turn professional after graduation. If Dixon gave them the cold shoulder, they would go peddle their school with the same routine to the next best recruit. *Rich man begging*, Dixon muttered to himself as he gritted his teeth and got out of his car.

Dixon trudged toward the house with his backpack. Once he reached the top step of the porch, Johnson and Coach Gardner arose to greet him. But before they could shake Dixon's hand, his mother darted forward.

"Look who came by to you see you, son," she said. "It's two of your favorite people."

Dixon suppressed the urge to roll his eyes again. He never liked it when she put words in his mouth, particularly those types of words. The two men standing in front of him weren't even on his list of people he liked; rather, they now held a special place on the list of people he despised.

Dixon forced a smile and extended his hand to Coach Gardner, whose hand had remained outstretched since the moment he stepped on the porch. Johnson then shook Dixon's hand as well before sitting down. Dixon leaned against the porch railing while Johnson and Coach Gardner returned to their respective seats. His mother excused herself and went inside.

"So, how are you doing, Dominique," Coach Gardner

began, "you know with Tre'vell's death and all?"

There were so many things Dixon wanted to say, but he stopped short. Without diplomacy, this meeting would get ugly.

"It's been tough," Dixon said. "I'm not gonna lie. I miss Tre'vell like crazy every day. He was an amazing friend."

"Do the police have any idea who would do this or why?" Coach Gardner asked.

Dixon shook his head. "Not yet anyway. But I'm sure they'll catch the scumbag who did this."

"Well, I just wanted to stop by and see how you were doing and find out if you were still going to keep your word that you were going to play for us," Coach Gardner said. "From what I understand, it was Tre'vell that wanted to re-nege on his commitment to play for Bryant, not you."

Dixon shrugged. "I'm not sure what I want to do any more. Tre'vell and I made a pact to go together, wherever we decided to go. But after visiting Bryant we decided to keep our options open."

Dixon delivered the half-truth to perfection. The whole truth was the recruits removed Bryant University from consideration. Yet, Dixon didn't want to tell them that just in case he didn't visit anywhere else he liked better. He doubted that would be the case since he had offers to visit half of the schools in the southeast. Based on his history with Bryant boosters and coaches, Dixon thought they would act like a stalker ex-girlfriend if he admitted the truth. But here they were on his front porch just days after he and Tre'vell had reneged on their commitment. Signing day couldn't arrive soon enough for Dixon.

"Well, I'm sorry to hear that, son," Coach Gardner said. "We had big plans for you. Still do, if you return to your senses."

Dixon nodded and looked down. He kept silent.

"Just think about what's best for your family. I under-stand if you think there's a better opportunity elsewhere, but I'm quite sure you won't find one. Don't let an opportunity like this slip away."

With that, Coach Gardner stood up and walked to the car. Johnson didn't get up as he eyed the coach. Once Coach Gardner's car door shut, Johnson leaned forward and spoke in a whisper.

"So, what did Alabama offer you?" Johnson asked. "You can tell me."

Dixon furrowed his brow and stared at Johnson. "I don't know what you're talking about."

"Oh, come on," Dixon said. "They didn't offer me nothin'. Get outta here with that talk."

"Look, I know something happened on your visit to Bryant that made you change your mind. And I think I know what it is. Don't play games with me. You're better off just shootin' me straight than lyin' to my face."

Dixon rolled his eyes and stood up. "I think we're done here. And you can tell Coach Gardner that I'm not inter-ested."

Johnson stood up as well. "You're going to regret this as long as you live."

Dixon stuck his chest out and cocked his head. He clenched his right fist as he glared at Johnson.

"Are you threatening me?" Dixon asked.

Dixon watched Johnson glance down at his fist before he answered. "No. I'm just trying to keep you from making the biggest mistake of your life."

Dixon unclenched his fist as Johnson walked off the

porch and toward his car. Dixon put his hands on the railing and leaned forward as he watched the pair drive away. He turned around when he heard the screen door bounce against the frame a couple of times.

"So, how'd it go?" his mother asked.

"Fine."

"Did you make a decision yet?"

"Yeah, I did."

"Really?"

"Yep. I decided I won't be going to Bryant."

CHAPTER 10

TUESDAY AFTERNOON CAL RAPPED on the screen door to Dominique Dixon's house. Mrs. Dixon answered the door.

"I don't think we were expecting anyone. Are you another coach?" she asked.

Cal shook his head. "No, ma'am. I'm a reporter from the Atlanta paper writing a story about what happened to Tre'vell Baker. I was wondering if I could ask Dominique a few questions."

"We're just finishin' up dinner. Have a seat out here in the porch and I'll go fetch him."

She disappeared inside and Cal chose one of the wooden chairs in desperate need of a paint job. Potter remained in the truck on a phone call, leaving Cal alone for the moment. Cal looked around at the surroundings. There were several clapboard houses nearby. A few chickens strutted around the area, meandering between the homes. Most of the cars parked in front of the homes looked like they belonged in another decade, if not century. Rust replaced missing swaths of paint. On one of the cars, a cinder block served as a stand-in for a missing tire.

Cal could hear the bayou stirring softly. A fall nip had

replaced the warm sun preparing to make its exit for the day. It seemed peaceful despite the apparent poverty of the people who lived in this area. One elderly man rocked in a chair on his front porch and waved at Cal. Cal waved back and enjoyed the serenity of the moment. Yet the calm was shattered when he heard the angry voice of a man yelling inside of Dixon's home.

Moments later, Dixon joined Cal on the front porch and shut the front door behind him.

"Sorry about that," Dixon said. "My dad can get a little grumpy at times."

Cal stood up and shook Dixon's hand. "No need to apologize. Cal Murphy from *The Atlanta Journal-Constitution*."

"Dominique Dixon. Nice to meet you, sir. My mom told me that you wanted to talk about Tre'vell Baker."

"Yeah, I'm writing a story on his death and was wondering if you could tell me more about him."

"Sure, what do you want to know?"

"I'd like to know what kind of guy he was."

Dixon didn't hesitate to answer. "Tre'vell was the best. He'd give you anything if you asked for it. He was always looking out for other people."

"What's something he did that shows that?"

"Well, there was a time when one kid on our team didn't have any cleats and his parents couldn't afford it. So, Tre'vell gave the kid his cleats."

"So, what did Tre'vell play in?"

"His sneakers. Caught eight passes that night and had a couple of touchdowns. Everybody was talking about it. The next Monday at practice, a new pair of cleats showed up in Tre'vell's locker."

"As I understand it, you guys were close, right?"

"Yeah, I gave him a ride home from practice every day. We went against each other in practice, which is why I think I developed the way I did. When you go against the best receiver in the state, maybe the best in the country, you're gonna get better."

"So, tell me about your trip to Bryant. What happened that made you change your mind?"

Before Tre'vell could answer, Potter wandered up on the porch. Cal watched Dixon eye the new guest before he clammed up.

"I'm not sure I want to talk about that."

"OK, anything else you can tell me about Tre'vell?"

"Nope, I think that covers it," Dixon snapped. "Look, I've got a lot of homework tonight so I need to get to it."

Dixon stood up and Cal followed his lead.

Potter stared at Dixon and deadpanned, "Is it my new cologne?" Then he cracked a smile. However, Dixon still appeared tense.

Potter led Cal back to the car. Just as Cal was about to get in, Dixon called out.

"Wait, Mr. Murphy!"

Cal sensed that Potter's presence made Dixon nervous. He hustled toward the porch, out of Potter's earshot.

"Yes?"

"There's more I want to tell you and something I want to show you. Meet me Thursday after school behind the Texaco station. But come alone."

"Will do. See you then."

Cal returned to the truck.

"What was that all about?" Potter asked as Cal climbed into the truck and buckled his seat beat.

"Just a kid trying to be polite."

"Did he have anything interestin' to say?"

"Not really. Just the same ole stuff everyone around here says about Tre'vell Baker. He's a good kid, would do anything for anybody, never had a better teammate. It's how people always speak of young kids who die. It's like they were flawless."

"You ever seen law enforcement dredge a river for a dead body?"

Cal shook his head.

"They bring out a barge that has a machine with grapplin' hooks on it that reaches down into the water and pulls up whatever's on the bottom. Most of the time, they don't find any dead bodies. But what they do find is often worse than the dead body itself."

Cal furrowed his brow and stared at Potter. "Your point?"

"My point is nobody likes to dredge up what's beneath the surface. Most people are content to let whatever is under there stay that way. No need muddyin' the water, if you know what I mean."

Cal nodded. "So, you're saying that nobody is going to tell me what Tre'vell Baker was really like?"

"People will say what they wanna say."

Frustrated with Potter's riddles, Cal didn't respond. He hoped the silence would entice Potter to say what he meant instead of talking in bayou riddles.

They rode for several minutes without a word being spoken before Potter couldn't help himself any longer.

"What I'm tryin' to say, Cal, is that you're not gonna solve Baker's murder by askin' his best friend what kind of guy he was or what his favorite food was or where he liked to eat or whatever it was that you were up there askin' Dixon.

Sometimes there are forces at work that we just don't understand."

Cal looked at Potter, who was pointing upward with his right index finger.

"You're saying God did this?"

"Who knows? Maybe it was just Baker's time to go."

"That might be a good enough answer for you, but not for me—or my editor. Speaking of which, I need to give him a call. Also, I need to get some batteries for my recorder. Can you pull into the gas station here so I can grab some?"

Potter veered his truck into the Texaco gas station parking lot and jammed the stick into park. "Take all the time you need."

Cal climbed out of the truck and pulled out his phone. He dialed his editor's number.

"Gatlin."

"Hey, Gatlin. It's Murphy. How are things going?" Cal leaned against the ice machine sitting outside the entrance of the store.

"Just like normal. The Braves' game is headed for extra innings and Tillman is late with his Hawks' feature. I swear I've never met anyone who labored over his words like him. My gosh, just send the dang story in already. It's not like anybody cares about that team anyway."

"So, it sucks, huh?"

"Like I said, it's another normal night at the paper. How are things going on your end?"

"Well, it's been an interesting day."

"Interesting enough to make for a good story."

"Still working on that. I've got a colorful local guide and have met quite a few people that have given me some good background on Tre'vell Baker. But I'm still searching for an angle."

"Well, don't go snooping around the bayou at night. I hear the gators down there have been known to eat a man whole."

Cal laughed. "You obviously haven't been down here if that's the tale you're hearing. I've already heard far more terrifying stories about gators—and baby gators at that."

"Be safe and check in tomorrow and let me know if anything noteworthy pops up. I think if this story pans out, we'll have a winner on our hands."

Cal hung up and went inside the story to buy some batteries. He eyed Potter, who was jabbering away on his phone.

Once Cal made his purchase, he pushed open the door and nearly hit an old man. "Excuse me, sir. Sorry about that," Cal said.

The old man stopped and stared at Cal. He hadn't shaved in quite some time and his clothes looked like something picked out of the Army surplus bargain bin. He wore a camouflage mesh cap with the bill pulled down just above his eyes.

"Hey," the old man said. "Are you that reporter guy snoopin' around here?"

Cal stopped. He glanced at Potter's truck where his guide was still yapping away on the phone. "Yeah, I'm from the Atlanta newspaper. How do you know that?"

"New travels fast around here. But I wanted to tell ya to be careful."

"Why's that? Am I doing something dangerous?"

"Could be. Just watch yer back."

Cal walked off and glanced back at the old man over his shoulder. The old man hadn't moved. He stood glaring at Cal.

Once inside the truck, Cal remained quiet as Potter

ended his call out of courtesy to his guest.

"So, ya got to meet old man Boudreaux?"

"Who is that guy?"

"Meanest man in a hundred miles of here. Rumor has it that he wrestled a bear to the ground and killed it with his bear hands. He knows where all the bodies are buried."

"Maybe that's why he told me not to go poking around."

"Yeah, he's scared of any outsider. He thinks they're out to get him. He's almost certifiable. But the people of Saint-Parran tolerate him. He's pretty harmless."

"He kind of creeped me out, to be honest."

"He'll do that to ya. But I've got a cure for that."

"Oh?"

"Yeah, Bons Temps is calling your name. You need a drink."

CHAPTER 11

ACCORDING TO POTTER, the water and woods surrounding Saint-Parran buzzed with activity during daylight. For fisher and hunters, the daylight hours were spent on the water with a rod and reel or in the swamps with a shotgun or rifle. But at night, everyone returned to Saint-Parran, unwinding at the ever-popular Bons Temps, the only bar within twenty miles. A wooden porch fronting the grey cinder block structure appeared vulnerable to a strong gust of wind, much less a hurricane. In 1965, the bar gained legendary status throughout the region when it survived Hurricane Betsy with barely a scratch. Rumors spread of Bons Temps' iron-clad walls, starting a tradition of hurricane parties there.

Drunk patrons unable to hold their tongues made for fantastic background sources. On occasion, they also provided great leads.

"This looks like the place to be," Cal said as they pulled into a gravel parking lot filled with outfitters' trucks and SUVs.

"It's the only place to be," Potter said.

As Cal pushed through the large wooden door, the place looked more like a dance club than a bar. In an open area at the center of the room, several couples twirled around to the rhythmic sounds of Zydeco music, a Louisiana tradition. Fiddles, accordions, and an unfamiliar song wailing from the jukebox drowned out the chatter between patrons sitting at nearby tables.

Cal felt Potter poke him in his back.

"Head left," Potter said.

Cal turned to his left and saw a small opening that led to another large room, one that had been added on. Instead of cinder block, the walls were made out of brick. The music switched to a Hank Williams Jr. song about a lying jukebox and followed them into the next room.

Potter stepped in front of Cal and headed straight for the lone empty table at the back of the room.

"Is this place always like this?" Cal said as he sat down.

"It is when there are a lot of fishermen in town," Potter answered. "It'll probably be like this until April or May when it thaws out up north. Saint-Parran is a great place to wait out Old Man Winter."

Cal motioned to the waitress to come over.

"What are you boys havin' tonight?" she asked. She worked over her gum while awaiting their response. Bright blue eyes and brown curly hair. She couldn't have graduated from high school more than a year ago.

"Two bottles of Abita Restoration Pale Ale, please," Potter said. "My friend here needs to try some real Louisiana beer."

"You got it, Uncle Phil," she said as she winked at Cal.

"That's your niece?" Cal asked after she walked away.

Potter nodded. "Little Cassidy. She's all grown up now. She's a real peach, the sweetest gal in Toulon Parish."

Cal glanced around the room and took in the scene. Men competed with the loud jukebox and each other in retelling their conquests for the day. Every few moments, Cal noticed men demonstrating the length of the fish they either caught or let get away. The length between their hands seemed to grow with each new tale. Cal chuckled to himself.

"What are you laughin' at?" Potter asked.

"This," Cal said, waving his hand across the room. "Everybody sitting around and telling stories about fishing."

"You mean, lies?"

"Yeah. At least, it looks that way from where I'm sitting."

"If there's one thing you learn to do down in the bayou, it's how to spin a good tale. Gotta pass the time somehow and real life ain't nearly as excitin' as everybody down here makes it out to be. We ain't all wrestlin' bears and giggin' frogs and tannin' gator hides every day. Most days, time moves about as fast as the water in the bayou. The hours drip by. Then we come here and make up stuff."

"It's like that everywhere," Cal said. He eyed Cassidy heading toward them with a pair of beers.

"There ya go, gentlemen. Enjoy." She put the beers on the table and scurried off to another table.

"You ever talk about anything else other than hunting and fishing?" Cal asked.

"Oh, yeah. We'll get into politics and sports and religion and the weather. The usual."

"Do most of these guys live down here?"

"Only for part of the year. Old men with money to burn. They buy a place down here and fish and hunt until they get tired of it. Then they sell their place and go somewhere else."

"What about that guy over there?" Cal asked as he nodded in the direction of Hugh Sanders.

"Hugh Sanders," Potter said with a hint of disgust in his

voice. "I wish he'd get tired of the bayou and move on."

"What's wrong with him?"

"He's a 'Bama fan, that's what. And a big booster."

"Let's invite him over," Cal said.

Before Potter had a chance to protest, Cal walked over to Sanders' table and introduced himself. Sanders stood up and excused himself from his neighbor at the bar and joined Cal and Potter.

Sanders sat down and extended his hand to Potter. Potter didn't move.

"Still bitter over that beat down the Tide gave your boys a few weeks ago?" Sanders said with a big smile.

Potter leaned back in his chair and waved off Sanders. "You're so dadgum annoyin', Sanders. You know that?"

Sanders smiled again and looked at Cal. "He's just jealous. We got their old coach and now they can't beat us. Ain't much worse than an angry Cajun."

"When was the last time Bama won the national title?" Potter shot back.

"Oh, that stupid new college football playoff. They keep putting Alabama against the best teams. It's rigged."

"Wait a minute. I thought Alabama was the best?"

Cal enjoyed the banter between the two rivals. Having grown up in the Northwest, great football rivalries were sparse and never this heated.

Sanders ignored Potter. "What brings you down to Saint-Parran, Cal?"

"Working on a story about recruiting."

"Let me guess—Dominique Dixon and Tre'vell Baker?"

Call nodded.

"It's a shame about that Baker kid," Sanders said as he shook his head. "He had a ton of talent and a world of potential. He could've been a superstar in the NFL one day. Too bad he never got a chance."

Potter nodded. "Yep, it's a tragedy."

"Potter here tells me you're a big booster at Alabama," Cal said to Sanders.

"Referring to my weight or my wallet?" Sanders quipped. "Yeah, I support Alabama. Always have. Always will."

"What do you think about the Dixon kid?"

"Heckuva athlete. I expect he'll wind up at Alabama. He's certainly not going to Bryant, that's for sure."

A voice then bellowed over their table that broke the flow of conversation. "Who's not going to Bryant?" It was Frank Johnson.

"Frank Johnson—I guess they stopped keepin' the riff-raff outta here," Sanders said.

"You would know since they actually let you in tonight," Johnson fired back.

Cal wondered if he had magically transported back to middle school. The banter between the men was no less juvenile than anything he experienced prior to the ninth grade. He suspected a game of pencil break, paper football, or rocks, scissors, paper would break out at any moment to settle the mindless debate.

Sanders stood up. "Well, gentlemen, I can see I've overstayed my welcome. Take care and don't believe a word out of this man's mouth." He patted Johnson on the back before returning to his table. He didn't look back, while Johnson made a face at him.

Uninvited, Johnson took Sanders' seat at the table and—after brief introductions—launched into a diatribe about how evil Hugh Sanders was and how he was a perfect microcosm for how vile the University of Alabama football

program was. He extoled the virtues of winning while playing by the rules. It amused Cal, especially since Bryant had
been placed on probation by the NCAA several times for
skirting the established guideline for recruiting practices.

Potter stared into his beer as Johnson droned on about
how great of a school Bryant was and how its athletic program excelled in every sport.

"Are you done yet?" Potter asked.

"No, I'm just getting started," Johnson answered.

Moments later, Cassidy returned to get Johnson's order
and bring refills.

Cal and Potter sat and listened to Johnson, who exuded
passion and fervor for his favorite college football team.
Johnson also explained how Dixon would be a fool to go to
Alabama—or anywhere else other than Bryant.

Cassidy returned with Johnson's food, which brought an
end to his uninvited soliloquy.

"Have you ever had boudin, Cal?" Johnson asked as he
doctored his meal with an array of spices already on the
table.

Cal shook his head.

"A friend of mine told me it would put hair on my chest.
Was he ever right!" Johnson said.

"What's in it?"

"You need to try it for yourself to find out. The real secret's in the spices. Better make sure you have a big glass of
beer nearby to quench that fire. I make mine so spicy it's li-
able to put a guy in the hospital if he's not man enough."

Cal shook his head and smiled as he watched Johnson
work his fork over the foreign dish. He didn't really want to
know what boudin was, much less put it in his mouth.

As they were finishing their meal, Johnson stood up to

leave. His not-so-concealed handgun caught Cal's eye.

"Is it that dangerous around here you need to carry one of those?" Cal asked, gesturing toward the gun.

"Oh, this?" Johnson asked as he patted the gun. "This is my Glock 42. An excellent firearm if you're looking for protection. It's got its drawbacks, like only holding six rounds in a clip, so you better be a good shot or have a fast getaway if you intend to get into a scuffle. But other than that, she's perfect. Can't have it all, can you?"

While Cal struggled to find a worthy response, Johnson broke into a hearty laugh. "It's not like that, Cal—I just keep it for protection from wildlife. You know, like gators and bears and flyin' fish with swords." He winked at Cal. "You fellas have a good evening."

Potter suggested it was time to get Cal back to his motel. "Another big day ahead for you tomorrow. You need a good night's sleep. Never know what will happen next in the bayou."

***

Hugh Sanders watched from his truck as Potter and Cal exited Bons Temps. He dialed a number on his cell phone and eyed the parking lot. The phone rang several times before someone picked up.

"I think we may have a problem," Sanders said.

He listened intently over the next few minutes to a set of instructions. When the speaker finished, Sanders nodded his head for no one but himself.

"I understand," he said. "I'll handle it." Sanders ended the call—the plan changed.

CHAPTER 12

CAL AWOKE WEDNESDAY to the buzzing alarm clock emanating from his phone. He squinted at his surroundings—a motel room still adorned with wallpaper from the 1970s. The brown shag carpets were a mess as well. The beige rotary phone dominated the bed stand. Time didn't just forget this place; it all but erased it.

The alarm chirped at Cal until he finally turned it off. He rubbed his face and looked at his cell phone for the time. It was 8:30 and he needed to check in with Kelly. But before he did, he noticed he had a voice message.

He played the message.

"Hi, Cal. This is Mike Nicholson from Nicholson and Associates. I hope you're doing well. I wanted to let you know that I just spoke with that publisher I was telling you about and he's off the market now. Barry Anderson called him with a great recruiting story and the publisher thinks that Barry's book will bale him out. In short, he doesn't need the story any more. Sorry to get your hopes up, but I can probably find somebody else who'll take it if it pans out and is any good. You just won't get the kind of money we were discussing. Hate to start your day off with a message like this, but that's how it is. Give me a call back if you have any questions."

Cal glared at his phone. Then he dropped it.

How can this be happening to me? I seriously can't catch a break.

Before Cal had long to ponder his predicament, his phone rang again. It was Kelly.

"Cal?" Kelly asked.

"Hey, Kelly. How are you?"

"Great!"

"That's good to hear. I've got something I have to tell you."

"No, I called you. I get to go first."

"OK, you first." Cal didn't mind the delay—until he heard the reason for her joy.

"I started looking through some magazines today and I found the perfect nursery set."

"That's great, honey. There's not something else you need to tell me, is there?"

"What? Like I'm pregnant?"

"I don't know. *Are* you?"

"No, but I know I will be."

"Well, I just thought from how chipper you sounded that maybe you had some good news for me."

"You don't think this is good news? I picked out our nursery already. That's huge news!"

"You're right, you're right. I know it is. I just hadn't heard you this happy in a while."

"Maybe I'm a little bit too hopeful today. I know you're going to land that big book deal that will help pay for my surgery and get our little family going."

"Yeah, that's—that's great, honey. I'm excited too."

"Super! So, what is it that you wanted to tell me?"

Cal paused for a moment. "I'm making some headway in this story."

"Figure out who did it yet?"

"Not yet, but I've met some colorful people down here."

"Any worth telling me about?"

"My favorite so far has been the honorable Sheriff Mouton, who eats nails for breakfast and spits one-liners out like it's his job."

"So he's better at that than his real job?"

"Well, considering he hasn't caught the person responsible for shooting Tre'vell Baker yet, I'd say so."

"Stay safe and have fun, honey. I've got to run to the store to pick up some paint for the nursery."

Cal ended the call and collapsed on the bed.

Could my day start any worse?

Cal's phone rang again. It was his editor, Jim Gatlin.

"Good morning, Cal," Jim said.

"Mornin'," Cal mumbled.

"Too much moonshine last night, Cal?"

"No, I just got crapped on, that's all."

"Well, you're about to get dumped on if those weather reports are true."

"What are you talking about?"

"That little tropical storm brewing in the Gulf that meteorologists said was heading for Mexico made a sudden turn north. Now, they're predicting it'll make landfall sometime Saturday evening. It's weak right now, but they think it's going to pick up steam."

"Oh, wonderful."

"If I were you, I'd try to get out of there as fast as you can. You don't want to be down there when a storm hits."

"What about my story?"

"I don't want you stranded down there. We'll figure something else out."

"OK, I'll call you back in a little while and let you know what's going on," Cal said before ending the call.

Cal needed to think. And he wasn't going to get any thinking done in his 1970s time capsule. He needed the best coffee in Louisiana to perk him up.

***

Cal meandered a quarter of a mile down the main strip before pushing open the door to Café Lagniappe. Aside from a couple of elderly gentlemen sitting in the corner, empty chairs and tables were the only things that filled the restaurant. Cal scanned the room for a place to sit, numb to the number of choices in front of him.

"You can sit anywhere you like," said a woman from behind the counter. At least Cal thought it was a woman. He couldn't actually see anyone, but he was sure that the voice was feminine. Then a woman popped up from behind the counter.

With a fishnet tied around her hair and an apron fastened around her waist, the waitress smiled at her new patron, revealing a mouth in severe need of dental work. Cal guessed the woman to be in her 50s.

She dug the pencil out from her hair and pulled her order pad out of her apron.

"You gonna just stand there or you gonna sit down so I can take your order?" she asked.

Cal decided to take a seat at the counter instead of sitting alone at a table.

"I hear the coffee is good here," Cal finally said.

"So you've been hangin' out with Potter?"

"What makes you think that?"

"He's the only person in Toulon Parish who brags about

the coffee here."

"Maybe Potter oversold the place. It's pretty much abandoned now."

The waitress slapped the counter with a towel. "Shoot. Between five-thirty and seven-thirty this place is hoppin'. After that, it is a ghost town."

"Why's that?"

"The early bird may get the worm, but the early worm gets the fish around here, if you know what I mean."

Cal figured it was a fishing analogy. All the colloquial expressions kept his mind sharp as he tried to figure out their meanings in context. He needed that coffee faster than she could pour it.

"First one in the water catches the most fish?" Cal asked.

"Something like that," she said as she slid a mug of steaming coffee in front of Cal. "I'm Gertie."

"Nice to meet you, Gertie. I'm Cal."

"So, Cal, what brings you to Saint-Parran? I know it ain't fishin'."

Cal chuckled. "Is it that obvious?"

"It'd only be more obvious if you wore a neon sign around your neck."

"Well, I'm a reporter and I'm here on assignment."

"Oh?"

"I'm writing about Tre'vell Baker and Dominique Dixon and about what it's like for two small town kids in the world of big time recruiting."

"Sadly, you're only writin' about one kid now."

"Yeah, I know. It's terrible. Did you know Tre'vell? Doesn't his mother work here?"

"Yes, I know Tre'vell—or knew him. And, yes, his mother *did* work here. Not any more."

"*Did* work here?"

"She just up and quit yesterday mornin'. Said she got a job out of town and was movin'."

"Where to?"

"She didn't say, but it is strange," Gertie said as she wiped the counter.

"How so?"

"That woman's been here as long as I can remember and she ain't never talked about movin'."

"Maybe she needs a fresh start or got a job somewhere else."

Gertie stopped wiping and looked at Cal. "You seriously think people like us interview for out-of-town jobs and get them? No. We just take whatever we can get wherever we can find it."

"You never know."

"But after all these years…" Gertie said. Her words hung in the air momentarily as if she were asking a question. "I heard her family came into some money. A cousin of hers won some harassment lawsuit. Maybe that's where she's going."

"Well, I was hoping to talk to her before she leaves."

"Oh, she's not going anywhere too soon. She still hasn't buried Tre'vell. That's tomorrow. And then after that, we're all gonna be gettin' outta here as quick as possible. That storm just might blow us off the map."

"I thought it was just a tropical storm."

"It was. But it just got upgraded to a category one hurricane." Gertie pointed at the television, which was covered by a weather map and a giant green circle blanketing the Gulf. "They're calling her Hurricane Phyllis and predicting she turns into a category three or four by the time she makes landfall."

"So everybody doesn't just go hang out at Bons Temps?"

"You've gotta stop listenin' to Potter. That guy's so full of it, his eyes are brown."

It was the first expression Cal heard that he knew exactly what it meant.

Cal fished out a ten-dollar bill and put it on the table.

"Thanks for the coffee, Gertie. Nice talking to you."

She smiled and nodded as Cal walked out the door. Now he had even more to think about.

CHAPTER 13

HUGH SANDERS JAMMED THE GEAR into park and hesitated to get out of his truck while sitting in Dominque Dixon's driveway. Being deep in Louisiana didn't mean Sanders had to miss his favorite sports talk radio program from Alabama any more, thanks to the advent of modern technology. He once beat a blue tooth to a pulp less than a day after he bought it. He still thought the word "twitter" meant "a bird chirping." And he believed that he could contract a physical virus from his computer that would put him in the hospital. But a podcast of the Paul Finebaum Show on his smart phone? "This is the kind of modern innovation that betters mankind," he told his friends more than once as he played episodes on his phone for them.

He remained riveted to his seat because Finebaum promised a call from "Ashley from Anniston." She was no "Phyllis from Mulga" when it came to expressing her passion for Alabama football, but she was a close second. Sanders thought Ashley's voice sounded much sexier and imagined her as a svelte Southern belle. If Sanders had ever bothered to look on his computer, he would've seen pictures that showed otherwise.

"… I'll tell you what, Finebaum, if those little bluebloods from Bryant think they're gonna just march into our state and start kickin' our butts all over the place, they've got another thing comin'. We are Alabama and we run this state. Everybody and their brother has taken a shot at us and we might get bloodied every now and then, but when it's all said and done, we're standin' and you're not. I garan-dang-tee you. Next year, we're gonna stomp a mud hole in Bryant and walk it dry. …"

Sanders pounded on his steering wheel and roared with laughter. "Now that's my kind of woman. Roll Tide," he said to himself, muttering Alabama's rally cry to a party of one. He closed the app and slipped his phone in his pocket before getting out of the truck. Before he got to the porch, Dixon was waiting for him.

"Two visits in the same week? What am I? A six-star recruit now?" Dixon asked.

"Don't let it go to your head," Sanders said.

"I still haven't made up my mind." Dixon looked down and kicked at the dirt.

"That's OK. Alabama hasn't made up their mind yet either. They got a cornerback from Dallas who they might sign instead. It's all about who commits first."

"I don't play that game. This is a big decision and I'm going to take my time."

"Time isn't your friend, son."

"Alabama would never renege on their offer to me. You and I both know that, so don't think pressuring me is gonna work."

"Think what you want. Coach Raymond is under a lot of pressure not to over-sign like he has in the past. More recruits than available scholarships gets the NCAA sniffin' around. And we don't like that. Things are a changin'."

"Nothin' ever changes in Alabama."

"When it comes to winnin' football games, maybe. But how we win games and how we get recruits is changin', whether you wanna believe it or not."

"I'm still not sure where I'm gonna go. I'm just not ready to decide."

"Sure. Take your time and think about your options. You can stay in state, go to LSU and eat crow. You can play for those hillbillies in Tennessee and maybe make it to a bowl game once in your career. Go to Texas and compete against lesser competition in that weak conference of theirs. Or, heck, go to Southern California, learn to surf, and play against teams that wear baby blue uniforms. Or you can go to Alabama where you belong and get a championship ring or two while playin' for the best coach in the country."

"You all say the same thing."

"There's only one Alabama—and there's not another team that's won as many national titles as we have in the past fifteen years. That's a fact."

It was an undeniable fact, the silver bullet Hugh Sanders kept locked and loaded in his chamber of comebacks for anyone who dared to suggest that Alabama had an equal in the college football universe. However, it was a fact best reserved for bar room debates rather than using it to berate a potential recruit.

Dixon looked back down at the ground again and didn't say a word. Sanders decided he needed to soften up before leaving.

"Look, you take your time," Sanders said. "But remember you don't have forever. Alabama will move on with or without you. And while I think you'll make Alabama a better team, one player does not make a championship. Don't forget that."

Dixon nodded. "I'll keep that in mind."

Sanders said his good-bye and trudged back to the truck. He wondered if he'd done more harm than good when it came to his assignment. He didn't care if Dixon decided to go somewhere else, but he still needed the star recruit to trust him if his plan was going to work.

CHAPTER 14

WHILE POTTER FISHED in the morning with a last-minute client, Cal spent that time making phone calls and surfing the Internet for more information about Tre'vell Baker and Dominique Dixon's recruiting journey. Nothing gave him any indication that Baker's death was related to his recruitment. Though nothing suggested Baker was involved in any suspicious activity either. The stalemate of information started to drive Cal crazy. He figured if anything was going to give him a clue as to the true nature of Baker's death, Lanette Baker could.

Once the afternoon rolled around, Potter met up with Cal for more chauffeur duty. Potter pounded on Cal's motel door, announcing his presence to Cal and several rooms on both sides.

Cal opened the door, holding only his small computer bag.

"You gonna beat down my door?" Cal asked.

"Just wanted to make sure you heard me."

"All of Toulon Parish heard you."

"All of Toulon Parish loves me."

"That's what you think," Cal said as he yanked the door open to Potter's truck.

"You been talkin' to Gertie, haven't you? That woman loves gossip more than life itself. She thinks it's fun to scare my clients with her so-called facts about me."

"She did a pretty good job."

"Well, she's full of it."

"Funny. She said the same thing about you."

Potter latched his seat belt and froze. He stared at Cal for a moment and shook his head. Then he turned the ignition as the truck roared to life.

"Don't believe everything you hear, Cal. There are a lot of snakes in the swamp."

***

Cal's first glimpse at the Baker place gave him an eerie feeling. Potter navigated his truck down the road that wasn't serviced by any transportation department. Teeth-jarring ruts and runaway tree roots dominated the only clear pathway to a set of houses set near the water.

"You ever been back here?" Cal asked.

"What do you think?" Potter said.

They continued on for another minute in silence. Cal took note of his surroundings. Painting the scene for readers served as a trademark of his features stories. The setting for this one would be important since it was the same location where Baker was killed.

Potter stopped the truck and put it in park.

"If it's all the same to you, Cal, I'm gonna sit this one out," he said.

"Fishing wear you out this morning?" Cal asked.

"You could say that."

Cal climbed out of the truck and began walking toward the Baker's house. The steps creaked beneath his feet as he walked up the porch. The screen door was the only barrier between him and the rest of the house. Unsure of whether to knock or call out, Cal did both at the same time.

"Hello? Is anybody home?"

He heard the scuffling of feet and hushed voices until a woman finally appeared at the door.

"Are you Cal?" she asked.

Cal nodded. "Mrs. Baker?"

"In the flesh," she said as she wiped her flour-covered hands on her cream-colored apron before offering to shake his hand. "You can call me Lanette."

Cal shook her hand.

"Thanks for taking the time to meet me. I didn't want to intrude on your grieving, but I've got to get out of here before the storm hits."

Lanette laughed nervously and dismissed his comment with the wave of her hand. "The storm? Ain't nothin' gets people worked up around here like the threat of a storm. I doubt we'll even see a drop of rain. Come on in."

The screen door creaked as it closed behind Cal and bounced several times against the doorframe. Cal glanced around the room at the banged up walls in need of a fresh coat of paint. Knick-knacks littered the place and only one picture rested on a small table near the entryway. It was a picture of Lanette and her boys.

"Is this Tre'vell?" Cal asked, pointing at the oldest-looking boy in the picture.

Lanette nodded. "We took that picture this summer at my family reunion. It was a wonderful day and we all had so much hope. It's hard to believe he's gone."

Cal studied Lanette's face. Hard lines around the corner of her eyes. Her brown eyes sparkled despite the fact that they looked red, either from nights of crying or hard days of work—or both. A rigid jawbone and a mouth full of teeth, most of which were crooked.

"Would you like some tea?" she asked. Without waiting for an answer, she waddled toward the kitchen.

She returned to the living room moments later with a fresh glass of iced tea in her hand. "Here you go, Cal. Have a seat."

Cal sank into the nearest sofa and set down his drink. He pulled out his pad and began flipping through his pages of notes. Lanette sat in a chair across from him and folded her hands in her lap.

"I am trying to get a better picture of who Tre'vell was and what he was like. Can you tell me about how he started playing football?"

"Tre'vell always loved football as long as I can remember. He'd always play with the neighbors or with his brothers in the backyard. But I remember the day he told us all he was going to be a football player."

"What happened?"

"The Blue Grass Miracle. You remember that play?"

"Was that when LSU beat Kentucky on a Hail Mary at the end of the game?"

"It wasn't just a Hail Mary—it was more than a prayer. On the last play of the game, Michael Clayton tipped a long pass from Marcus Randall, and somehow Devery Henderson caught it and ran it in for a touchdown. The whole bayou was shoutin' like somebody got stabbed. It was crazy."

"And you remember all that so well?"

"Honey, we've all seen that play so many times down here I can describe the trainers handing out water during the timeout before the play. That game's legendary in these parts."

Cal remembered seeing the highlight on one of those countdown shows on the most shocking comebacks in college football. But it wasn't as familiar to him as it was to Lanette.

"So, that's when he decided he wanted to play football?"

"I think every kid under the age of eighteen in the state of Louisiana decided they wanted to play football for LSU if they hadn't already. But Tre'vell made a big deal out of it. He drew a picture of himself wearing LSU colors with the number nine on his jersey. He wanted to be just like the player who scored the touchdown."

"I've heard a lot of great things about Tre'vell as a person. What made him so special to you?"

"A couple of years ago, we were in a rough spot. We didn't have no money and barely had enough food. But Tre'vell didn't complain once. For about a month, he barely ate. He'd give up his meal for his brother to have seconds."

"Sounds like a great kid."

Lanette nodded in agreement. "The best."

"So, what kind of progress has the sheriff made in his investigation?"

"Sheriff Mouton? That man's worthless when it comes to solving crime."

"I heard he was one of the best at solving cases."

"Maybe if he's there when two men start shootin' at each other."

"He came around here once but he said it was probably just some freak stray bullet."

"Do you believe him?"

Lanette rubbed her hands together and looked at the floor. "I can't imagine anybody would want to kill him. He didn't have any enemies."

"So you don't think his death could've had anything to do with the fact that he reneged on his commitment to Bryant University just a few days before?"

"People are serious about their football around here, but not serious enough to kill anybody over it—unless they're drunk at Bons Temps maybe."

Cal sensed he wasn't getting anywhere with Lanette. He nodded and jotted down some more notes.

"Now, I don't mind these questions, but you didn't say you were tryin' to figure out who killed Tre'vell," she said.

"I'm sorry, Lanette. I didn't mean to offend you."

She waved her hand at Cal. "It's not going to offend me—it's just that I'm ready to move on from the whole thing after tomorrow and don't want to get it drug up again."

"I understand. So, what's next for you? Is it true that you're moving?"

"Yeah. I got a cousin who's helpin' me get a job. She promised it'd be a better life than what I've got here."

"So, where are you off to then?"

"Out of the bayou," she said.

Lanette's terse response let Cal know that it was time to stop asking about this and move on. "Well, I appreciate all your time and answering some tough questions. Your son has been quite an inspiration to me even though I've never met him. Sounds like you raised a great kid."

Lanette nodded. "Don't know how much I had to do with it, but he was somethin' else. I can't imagine a day will go by when I won't remember him."

Cal thanked Lanette and got up to leave. He glanced at a stack of letters on the entryway table next to the lone family photo. Most of the letters splayed about looked like stationary from college coaches addressed to her son.

But the letter on top was addressed to "Cousin Lanette" in messy handwriting. Cal noticed what looked like a check sticking out of the top. He couldn't make out the city on the return address, but it was from somewhere in Alabama.

Cal slipped back into the truck and didn't say a word to Potter.

CHAPTER 15

JIM GATLIN GAVE HIS REPORTERS plenty of leeway while they gathered their stories. He created such a big slush budget that his writers always felt confident they could get the necessary resources to properly report a story. It's part of the reason why Gatlin racked up so many Associated Press Sports Editors awards. Five years ago, he ran out of room to secure them to his office walls. He started rotating the plaques until he just decided to leave the most recent year's awards up. His walls were always full.

But Cal, with all his own truckloads of writing awards for past work, had yet to earn Gatlin and the paper any significant awards. Gatlin had been around long enough to know that award-winning writing was the result of three things: wordsmith skills, reporting prowess, and luck. So far, Cal's hunches fizzled into well-read pieces, but nothing that was going to earn the Atlanta newspaper's sports staff another honor.

Gatlin dialed Cal's number. He needed an update of his whereabouts. With the story likely going nowhere, Gatlin needed Cal back in Atlanta to help cover a pre-season Hawks game. The regular beat reporter for the Hawks fell ill with a stomach virus and everyone else was either covered up with assignments or not scheduled to work. Overtime was no longer a luxury the paper afforded any reporter, even an editor with a slush fund like Gatlin's.

Cal answered, plugging his other ear as he scrambled to escape the party-like atmosphere of Bons Temps.

"Sounds like a party going on there, Cal," Gatlin said.

"Just taking it easy tonight. I've got a lot to think about."

"Got anything to write about?"

"Not yet. I'm still working on it."

"Well, I think I warned you about the storm coming."

"Some of the locals think it's nothing. Besides, I feel like I'm close to discovering some dark secrets around here."

"It's the bayou, Cal. There are dark secrets lurking everywhere."

"Not like this. I feel like everyone is sketchy, like it could be any one of a handful of people I've spoken with. Nobody seems like they're being up front with me."

"Why should they be? You're some big city reporter."

"It's like they're all covering it up."

"Well, we don't have any more time to uncover anything. I need you back in Atlanta to cover the Hawks on Saturday. I already booked you a flight home for tomorrow afternoon."

"Oh, come on, Gatlin. I'm supposed to talk with the Dixon kid tomorrow. He sounded like he had something important to tell me. Besides, this is the first story I've had in a while with some real potential."

"Why do you say that?"

"I say it because it's true. You've assigned me nothing that matches my potential as a reporter—just bush league stuff. But this is the kind of story I thrive on. It brings out the best in me."

Gatlin paused for a moment to think. He needed Cal to come up with a winning story far more than he needed him to cover a meaningless pre-season basketball game.

"Fine. It's the Hawks. There won't be five hundred people there anyway and even fewer interested in reading about it the morning after. I'll get some intern to cover it."

"You won't be sorry."

"I better not be. What's going on tomorrow?"

"Tre'vell Baker's funeral. I should be able to interview a few more people afterward."

"I expect a full report tomorrow. And don't ignore that storm, Cal. It's still bearing down on Louisiana."

Gatlin hung up, unsure if he made the right decision. He trusted Cal even though his young hotshot reporter had done nothing in Atlanta to earn his trust.

CHAPTER 16

DOMINIQUE DIXON AWOKE from one dream to another on Thursday morning. His mother knocked on his door and called his name, as was their customary ritual. But there was something different in her voice.

"Nique, time to get up!" she said in a sing-song manner. She normally grunted or yelled at him. But this time her voice surprised him. "There's a surprise for you."

Dixon shot out of bed and scrambled to put on his sweat pants and a t-shirt. The last time his mother told him about a surprise she gave him tickets to see the Saints play the Falcons in New Orleans. She never told him where the tickets came from, but he never asked. He didn't want to ruin a good surprise. On Sunday, the Saints were playing the 49ers—a fact Dixon knew all too well.

"Good mornin', mom," he said.

"Mornin', son," she said. "How'd you sleep?"

"Good. What's goin' on?"

"What do you mean?"

"You said there's a surprise for me."

"Look outside."

Dixon walked to the window and pulled back the curtains. In the driveway sat a brand new red Audi TT.

Dixon put his hand over his mouth, agape from the shock. "Are you for real? When did you get that?"

"I didn't get it—and it's not for me."

Dixon's eyes widened. "What?"

"It's from your uncle."

"Uncle Bernard?"

"That's what it said on the note," she said, waving the note above her head.

"Gimme that." Dixon snatched the note from his mom's hands and read it.

> *I'm so proud of you, Dominique. You're big time now and I want to make sure you arrive at college in style. Good luck! ~ Uncle Bernard*

"Where'd he get the money for this?" Dixon asked.

"It's a gift, son. Just receive it and don't ask too many questions."

Dixon looked at his mother and then stared back down at the card. He had plenty of questions, starting with the fact that this wasn't his uncle's handwriting. But maybe his mother was right. The fewer questions, the better. The less he knew, the more likely he wouldn't get in trouble for taking a gift—a gift he knew never came from his real uncle Bernard.

***

Saint-Parran High buzzed Thursday morning over Dixon's new vehicle.

"So, when are we going to shoot a rap video of you and a bunch of girls in bikinis all over you in this car?" asked Carl Nelson.

Dixon shook his head. "No need for all that."

"Seriously? No need to make you look like the stud that you are?"

"It's just a car," Dixon said as he tried to downplay the gift.

"Just a car? If I didn't know any better, I'd have thought you lost your mind."

"How so?"

"This is your dream car. You talk about this car all the time. And now it suddenly shows up in your driveway as a gift from your uncle. We've got to make an epic video, spliced with highlights of you intercepting a pass and returning it for a touchdown. You'd have colleges beggin' you to go play for them."

"I already do, Carl."

"I mean schools like Southern Cal and Ohio State and Miami."

"They've all sent me letters."

"And you're not going there?"

"I still haven't decided."

"Maybe you ought to find out who gave this to you and show them some loyalty."

"My uncle gave it to me," Dixon said as he looked at the ground and kicked at the pavement.

"I understand code, bro. It's all right. You don't have to tell me who gave it to you."

"I told you—my uncle gave it to me."

"No, it's cool."

Dixon grew frustrated with the suspicion from his friend—and everyone else for that matter. Before the first period bell rang, he had posed by his car with at least a dozen of his friends. Friends posted the picture on social media accounts with a short note about how Dixon's uncle gave him the car. The word *uncle* was always surrounded by quotation marks. By the time the second period bell rang, the hash tag "#MyUncleGaveIt2Me" was trending on Twitter in

Louisiana, Alabama, Mississippi, Florida, Texas, and Georgia.
Even Gatlin saw it.

***

Saint Anne's Catholic Church bustled with well-wishers and mourners. Cal, joined by Potter, estimated two hundred people jammed the pews to watch Tre'vell Baker receive a proper memorial before the private burial service. He also noted that both Hugh Sanders and Frank Johnson attended the service, as did a pair of assistant coaches from LSU.

Father Benoit opened the service and spoke about Baker's penchant for helping others. Everything he said seemed consistent with what Cal had heard in his interviews so far: Tre'vell Baker was an outstanding kid who put others above himself. He also shared a funny story about how Baker loved his iPhone and he was always the first person he turned to when looking for suggestions for apps. As a result, he mentioned how Lanette Baker thought it was best that her son be buried with his phone.

The service continued with a rendition of "O Sacred Heart, O Love Divine," sung fervently by all those in attendance. Next came a handful of Baker's friends and adult mentors—coaches and teachers—who praised the young man.

Father Benoit then resumed his position at the front of the church and delivered a stirring message about how everyone must make his life count and how no one ever knows when it will be his last day on earth. Cal wondered if maybe the stray bullet theory was true—it was all just a random incident. And a tragic one at that. Cal struggled to conceive why anyone would want to kill such a kid.

But then again, as an investigative reporter he knew that everyone had secrets.

CHAPTER 17

AFTER THE MEMORIAL SERVICE, Cal accompanied Potter to Café Lagniappe for some coffee. Everyone there recalled stories of Baker helping them or making a spectacular catch to win a football game for Saint-Parran High. Cal hoped to glean something more about Baker, though it sounded like more of the same.

Cal's phone buzzed. It was Gatlin.

"Sorry, I gotta take this," he said as got up out of his chair and walked outside.

"Hi, Gatlin," Cal said as he answered the phone.

"Cal, what are you doing down there? Are you drinking? Are you fishing? Please give me an excuse I can live with."

"Whoa, whoa. Slow down. What's going on?"

"Have you not been checking your email?"

"I've been at Tre'vell Baker's funeral service all morning."

"That's no excuse."

"No excuse for what?" Cal asked as he paced about the parking lot.

"No excuse for one of my reporters being on site for one of the biggest recruiting stories that's trending on Twitter right now—and not a single word of copy written about it," Gatlin said. Cal was glad several hundred miles separated him from his boss.

"I'm afraid I don't know what you're talking about."

"I'm talking about Dominique Dixon and that new Audi TT of his."

"What? I was just there. He didn't have an Audi."

"He does now. Just look up the hashtag MyUncle-GaveIt2Me on Twitter," Gatlin said. "Tell me what you see."

Cal put Gatlin on speakerphone so he could continue the conversation while he searched for the hashtag on the social media site.

It didn't take long for Cal to find the original source and gasp—first at the brazen nature of the initial tweet and then at the avalanche of responses.

First, there was a picture of Dixon flashing the peace sign next to his new Audi TT with the hashtag: #MyUncle-GaveIt2Me.

The reactionary nature of college football fans made social media sites a dangerous place. Bitter and jealous fans would turn a harmless tweet into a piranha feeding in the Twitter fishbowl. And since plenty of fans believed there was some shady business going on, embittered fans of southern college football teams united. The #MyUncleGaveIt2Me went viral with people taking pictures of themselves outside giant houses or nice cars, most of which didn't belong to them. It questioned the integrity of Dixon's tweet as well as attracted the attention of an NCAA investigator. By the early afternoon, one recruiting website had a story up quoting a kid at the school who said he knew for a fact an Alabama booster gave the car to Dixon.

And Cal hadn't written a single word about it, much less knew about it.

"I can get something on this for you," Cal said.

"No! It's too late for the world we live in. This isn't the 1990s. Besides, I want you on a plane tonight. You're gonna put some kind of story together—and then you're gonna be covering the Hawks this weekend. Got it?"

Cal hung up and trudged back into the café. He texted Dixon and told him he couldn't meet today and that he might not be back.

"Problems?" Potter asked as Cal sat back down.

"I've got to get back to Atlanta. Stuff in the office needs my attention."

Potter smiled. "All the more fishin' and huntin' for me this weekend."

"I'm glad one of us is happy."

"I'll get my keys."

CHAPTER 18

MOST DAYS FRANK JOHNSON would scream and curse over such an intrusion into his day. But today was different. His plan to spend all day Thursday fishing ended when Tre'vell Baker died. Thursday was the funeral and he decided he needed to be there. What he didn't plan on was the frenetic pace with which Dominique Dixon drew the watchful eye of the college football world with his new car.

But he didn't mind. This was opportunity, an opportunity that sent him scrambling to get his jet in Huntsville back south so he could win the day—or make sure that Alabama lost it.

His plane landed and came to a halt outside of his hanger. After a few moments, the cabin door opened and Guy Lewis stepped into the muggy bayou air.

"Is this really necessary?" Lewis said as he gestured at his clothes. Lewis sported a crimson-colored outfit—jogging pants, jacket, baseball cap. A diamond-studded necklace with a gold "A" jangled from his neck.

Johnson nodded. "It's what Alabama's gaudy fans wear." Johnson surveyed Lewis a moment before adjusting his cap. "Here, this is too straight," he said as he tugged it off-kilter. "No Alabama fan puts their cap on straight. You'd be a dead giveaway for an impostor."

"You sure this is gonna work?" Lewis asked.

"As long as you talk like an ignorant redneck, it'll work just fine. Trust me." Johnson pointed toward the vehicle awaiting Lewis. It was a white Yukon with spinning rims and an Alabama window sticker that spanned the length of the back window.

"Seriously?" Lewis asked.

"You gotta look the part."

Lewis rolled his eyes and shuffled toward the vehicle. He got inside and rolled down the window.

"The directions are on your seat there along with a picture of Dixon," Johnson said as he leaned on the door. "He should be easy to spot. Just look for the kid getting out of a red Audi TT at the Texaco station in about twenty minutes. Tell him you want to meet after practice and he will."

Lewis nodded. "You owe me big time for this."

Johnson slapped the side of the Yukon as Lewis drove away.

***

Cal thanked Potter for his help as he gathered his belongings and prepared to get on a flight headed for Atlanta.

"I couldn't have done it without you, Potter," Cal said.

"Aw, it was nothing. I'm sorry you didn't find out who did it. That would've made a heckuva story."

"It sure would have. Take care."

"You too—and you know where to find me if you need me any time soon." Potter gave him a hand-written receipt and waved.

Cal walked toward the ticket counter. He wasn't ready to leave. He'd only felt like he was just getting started.

How will I explain this to Kelly?

Cal's phone rang.

Speak of the devil.

"Hi, honey. How are you?" Cal answered.

"Excited to hear that you're coming home early. I got your message."

"Yeah. I'm excited to see you too—but not to be leaving so early."

"Did you not get everything you needed?"

"Not even close."

"Maybe you can go back down there soon."

"We can only hope."

"What are you suggesting? That the book deal is dead?"

Cal shifted from one foot to the other, thinking about the most delicate way to present the bad news. "Maybe. But I still have a chance. I just might need to make another trip down here."

He hated exaggerating with Kelly, but he couldn't break her heart. Not after she'd repainted the nursery while he was gone. Not after this was their big chance to get the money they needed to start a family.

"We'll talk about it when I get home," Cal added.

He knew they'd talk about it and it wouldn't be a fun conversation.

***

At the Texaco Station after school, Guy Lewis waited patiently for Dominique Dixon to arrive. Just as Johnson predicted, Dixon walked into the store ten minutes after school wrapped up for the day. Lewis leaned against the wall, waiting for the star athlete. Finally, Dixon appeared.

"Dominique, can I have a word with you?" Lewis said.

Dixon's head snapped toward the direction of Lewis'

voice. "Excuse me?"

"You are Dominique Dixon, right?"

Dixon nodded.

"Well, you're who I want to speak with," Lewis said.

"Oh?"

"Yeah, I had a few things to discuss with you."

"Wow. Another booster? You guys must be pretty desperate."

"We're never desperate. We just know what we want."

"Like the best cornerback in the country?"

"Something like that."

"Okay. I'm listening. But before you begin, I just wanted to say thanks for the car."

Lewis put his index finger to his mouth. "If you want to call me Uncle Bernard, I don't mind. But let's keep it our little secret."

While Lewis acted like their meeting was secretive, he wanted the exact opposite. He wanted complete transparency, the kind Johnson could capture on his phone and post on social media.

CHAPTER 19

CAL TRUDGED INTO HIS APARTMENT, dreading his confrontation with Kelly. While he was glad to reunite with his wife, admitting the truth wouldn't be easy. He smelled dinner on the table.

Kelly scurried into the front hallway as soon as she heard the door close behind Cal.

"You're home!" she said as she laid eyes upon him.

"In one piece, believe it or not," Cal answered.

"It is hard to believe with all those shady dealings that happen in the swamp."

Cal laughed. "It's not like that—but it is a different world."

"Hopefully a world you were able to capture a good story from to write a book about."

Cal said nothing.

"Come here, I want to show you the nursery."

Kelly dragged Cal down the hall into their spare bedroom, which was now an assortment of neutral baby colors.

"What do you think?"

"I think you did a great job while I was gone."

"Now all we need is for you to write that book."

"Kelly, there's something I need to tell you."

Kelly stared at Cal, awaiting the next words out of his mouth. "Well, what is it?"

"It's about the book deal."

"Have you signed a contract yet?"

Cal paused. "Not yet, but soon."

"Better hurry up. I'm getting antsy."

Kelly skipped off to the freshly painted baby room. Cal stood in the hallway, wondering if he could ever regain control of the lie he'd unleashed.

***

Cal sifted through his notes and couldn't come up with anything substantial. All the interviews, all the background, all the facts. Nothing led to a killer. It seemed as though Tre'vell Baker had nothing to hide.

Why would anyone kill him?

Cal's phone buzzed. It was Saint-Parran High School's football coach, Hal Holloway.

"Did I catch you at a bad time?"

"There's no good time for me these days."

"I only wanted to tell you this so you can stop one of these scumbags down here from ruinin' another kid's life. I can call you back—"

"No, no. I've got time for you. What you got?"

"After practice today, Dominique told me some Alabama booster approached him and talked to him. He said the guy wasn't discreet or anything and seemed like he wanted to be out in the open."

"Did the guy say who his name was?"

"They never do. Anyway, Dixon thanked the booster for the car and he told him to keep it a secret. Now he's a little concerned how it might look."

Even though Holloway couldn't see the reporter he was talking to, Cal nodded. But Cal wasn't sure it was a lie. Nothing about this story came in a straightforward manner.

Holloway continued. "I asked him to describe the man and when he did, it made me think about a story I heard several years ago about a Bryant University booster posing as an Alabama booster in an effort to get Alabama in trouble with the NCAA for rules violations. One of the kids snapped a picture of them talking. I'm sending it to you now along with the one from several years ago of the alleged Alabama booster who was caught giving recruits things in an effort to get the crime pinned on Alabama. I showed the picture to Dixon and he said it looks like the same guy. I've got all the information in the email for you. Whatever is going on, it seems shady."

Cal thanked the coach and hung up.

When Cal's email alerted him to the arrival of a new email, he opened it and began studying the pictures.

"Kelly!" he yelled. "I need your help."

CHAPTER 20

HUGH SANDERS PARKED HIS TRUCK right in front of Dominique Dixon's new red Audi TT in the school parking lot. The sun started to slip beyond the horizon and a cool November nip took to the air. Sanders rested against his truck and waited for Dixon.

Within minutes upon arriving, a stream of Saint-Parran High football players spilled into the parking lot toting their pads and helmets. Dixon was engaged in a conversation with one of the players, laughing and joking until another player ran up and showed Dixon something on his phone. In an instant, Dixon's face dropped. The playful banter ended. Dixon waved them off and walked alone toward his car.

"I'm surprised to see you here," Dixon said to Sanders as he reached his car. "Two of you in one day? Unbelievable. I can't even believe I'm still on your radar."

"There's still room for you at Alabama."

"Really? After Tyler Anderson committed today?"

"That cornerback out of Dallas?"

"Don't act like you don't know who he is."

Sanders knew exactly who he was. He also knew that Anderson pledged to attend Alabama next season only an hour ago. "You think Alabama is satisfied with one safety?"

Dixon shook his head. "I'm not sure what satisfies anybody these days."

"I can tell you what satisfies Alabama—that's winning championships. Anything else is a failure. I think that's why Coach Raymond likes you so much. He thinks that's the kind of young man you are, too." Sanders let his words hang in the air for a moment. "Is he right?"

Dixon took a deep breath and looked down. The top recruit appeared to give the question serious thought.

Before he could answer, Sanders proceeded. "Now that you've heard the news, I must let you in on a little secret: Alabama still wants you. But now that they've got Anderson locked up, they can walk away from you. They'd like you, but they're not willing to do anything to get you, if you know what I mean."

"Like give me a car?"

"Yeah, like that. But we don't do that for anybody."

"So did you come to take the car back?"

"I don't know who you've been talking to, but nobody associated with Alabama helped arrange this car for you."

"That's not what the guy told me before practice."

"What guy?"

Dixon shook his head. "Whatever, man. I'm not going to talk about this any more."

"Look, I came to tell you that the offer from Alabama is still good, but it comes with conditions now."

"Conditions?" Dixon asked.

"Yeah, like we need you to do something for us."

"Like what?"

Sanders paused and took a deep breath. This was the real reason he was here speaking with Dixon. It was the only reason why Dixon still mattered to Alabama. "We need to know what made you change your mind about playing for Bryant."

Dixon stared at Sanders. "I don't know what you mean."

"Oh, I think you do. It's no secret what Bryant was doing for both you and Tre'vell. But something happened and there are a few people at Alabama who want to know what it is. If you're willin' to explain yourself, there's still a scholarship for you at Alabama. There's likely a championship ring in it for you, too. More than what any other school can guarantee you."

"It just wasn't the right place for us."

Sanders shook his head and smiled. "You got a lot to learn, kid. I sell cars for a livin'—used cars. And I know when somebody's lyin' to me. You have yourself a good day. Best of luck with whoever will take you. Of course, you know how to reach me if you change your mind and decide you wanna tell me the truth."

Sanders nodded and climbed into his truck before driving away.

***

Dixon put his pads in his equipment bag and placed it in the trunk. Then he climbed into his car and stared at his phone.

Twelve text messages?

He scrolled through the messages one by one. He started to cry. Each message contained an apology from the various coaches who pursued him for his talents only days ago.

I'm sorry to tell you this, Dominique, but we've just fulfilled our quota for cornerbacks at Florida State.

There were similar messages from coaches from South Carolina, Georgia, Auburn, Arkansas, Florida, Louisiana State. The list went on and on.

What is this? What did I do?

Then Dixon looked at his Twitter feed. He put his hand over his mouth as he scanned the messages.

@NiqueBaller2 Good luck at junior college next season

@NiqueBaller2 Reggie Bush's uncle gave him an Audi TT too #toxic

@NiqueBaller2 Was there cash in the trunk? #sorryimnotsorry

@NiqueBaller2 Ignore those jealous punks … you gotta get it while you can #yolo

@NiqueBaller2 Sellout! You would've looked great in orange and blue #gogators

Dixon tried to blink back the tears that welled up in his eyes. All he'd worked for was vanishing right in front of him. Every scholarship. Every dream. Gone in the time it took to post a picture of his new car.

He opened a web browser on his phone and surfed to a recruiting website which contained a short story about him on the front page.

Toxic Bayou?

Almost overnight, five-star recruit Dominique Dixon went from top-flight recruit to toxic when a post of him and a new sports car went viral earlier today. Sources say that almost all the colleges that offered Dixon a scholarship are no longer interested due to the social media faux pas.

While Dixon isn't the first player to squander a chance to play at a major college program due to missteps on social media, his story is one of the harshest cautionary tales.

Dixon seethed as he glared at his phone.

"I'm not playin' at some junior college in the sticks in front of fifty people."

He slammed his fist on his steering wheel. He pressed the ignition button and the engine roared to life. It then purred before he jammed the stick into first gear and barked the tires.

He needed to call Sanders.

CHAPTER 21

"WHAT IS IT, HONEY?" Kelly asked as walked into the room. "I just finished making dinner. Can it wait?"

Cal shook his head. "Not if you want me to land that book deal."

Her face lit up. "How can I help?"

"I need you to enhance a picture taken by a camera phone."

"Cal, I'm a photo journalist, not a miracle worker."

"Just see what you can do to get a better resolution on this image. I'm emailing it to you now."

"OK, but no promises." She left the room to retrieve her laptop.

Cal read through his notes for the next fifteen minutes before Kelly returned carrying her laptop.

"Could you do it?" Cal asked.

Kelly winked at him. "Does a kitty cat have climbing gear?"

"Seriously? You? The south has taken hold of you already? Nobody down here can answer me straight. It's always some strange colloquial expression."

"What's got your panties in a bunch?"

Cal cut his eyes at Kelly and snarled.

"You know you love me," she said. "And you'll love me more after you see this."

She pushed the laptop in front of Cal, who stared at the image spread across the screen. Kelly managed to enlarge the picture while maintaining vital details. Not a single feature on the alleged Alabama booster's face was lost.

"Brilliant! You are amazing!"

"Yeah, yeah. Wait until you taste the chicken cordon bleu I made for us tonight."

Cal smiled. "Give me a few more minutes and I'll join you."

Kelly left the room as Cal picked up his cell phone and began dialing.

"Is Barry Hunter there?" Cal asked when someone answered.

"Speakin'. Who's this?" the man asked.

"This is Cal Murphy from *The Atlanta Journal-Constitution*. I'm working on a recruiting story and I heard you were an expert when it came to identifying boosters of college football programs in the south."

"The midwest and southwest, too," Hunter corrected.

"Excellent. I have a picture I want you to look at. I have a hunch there's some dirty dealings going on with a recruit I've been following and I was wondering if you could confirm if a guy in a picture is affiliated with Alabama or not."

"Only if you keep my name out of it."

Cal agreed and then wrote down Hunter's email address. In a matter of seconds, Cal emailed the photo and waited on the phone.

"That dirty dog," Hunter said.

"What? Do you know who that is?"

"Guy 'the snake' Lewis. He's dirtier than two ticks

mud-wrestlin' in an outhouse.''

"What does he do?"

"I don't know what his real job is, but he moonlights as a fake booster for hire. You want to pin somethin' dirty on a program, you call Guy Lewis. He'll dress up in just about anybody's team colors and do some dirty dealin' for the right price—except maybe Bryant University's."

"Is he a Bryant booster?"

"Nobody knows for sure. But I know of at least ten schools that he's done this to in the south—and Bryant ain't ever been among 'em. But this is a bit surprisin'."

"How so?"

"Nobody normally gets this close to him to take a picture."

"Kids and their cell phones these days."

"I reckon. But it's sloppy, even for Guy. He usually wants to give off the illusion that he's representin' a team. I don't think he wants his face associated with this. Bad for business."

Cal thanked Hunter for his help and hung up. He immediately began a web search for Guy Lewis and came up with several images that confirmed what Hunter said. Cal didn't doubt for a second that the man depicted in the photo talking to Dixon was Guy Lewis.

Cal walked into the kitchen and sat down at the table. A half-eaten chicken breast stuffed with ham and Swiss cheese sat on Kelly's plate.

"Hungry?"

"Famished. What did you find out?"

"I've got a question for you first."

"What's that?"

"Do we have any mileage we can use for a plane ticket?"

"What on earth do you need that for?" Kelly said as she put down her fork.

"I have to level with you, Kelly. I need to go back to Louisiana."

"The paper's not going to pay for it?"

"Gatlin took me off the story permanently," Cal said as he sat down.

"What?"

"Yeah, he didn't think there was anything there."

"What about your literary agent? Can't he help pay for it?"

"Uh, not exactly."

"What exactly do you mean?"

"I mean, the publisher found another story to publish and cut me loose. I'm on my own."

Kelly broke down and started sobbing. Cal walked over to comfort her but she pushed him away.

"Leave me alone. I should've known this was going to happen. I'm never going to get pregnant."

"Honey, it's just a temporary setback. It'll work out."

Cal returned to his seat and ate his dinner over Kelly's quiet cries. He couldn't bear to see her in such emotional pain. But he wasn't ready to give up on the story either.

CHAPTER 22

DOMINIQUE DIXON SAT SLUMPED against the cinder block wall of the Saint-Parran High field house as he waited for Hugh Sanders. The hum of the light on the utility pole and the cacophony of croaking bullfrogs created a soundtrack to accompany the nip in the evening air. Dixon snatched a swatch of grass and picked at it as he pondered the recent events in his life. A tear streaked down his face. He sniffled and wiped the tear away with the back of his hand.

"Everything all right?" a man asked as he appeared from around the corner. It was Hugh Sanders.

"Yeah, everything's fine," Dixon answered as he stood up.

"You've been through a lot lately. I think anyone would understand being a little emotional after all you've been through."

"I'm fine."

"If you were fine, we wouldn't be here. The truth is everything you worked for is crumbling. I hope we can rectify that situation for you."

Dixon seethed inwardly but put on a pleasant demeanor for Sanders as if his future depended on it.

"I hope so, too."

"So what have you got for me?"

"The smoking gun on Bryant University."

"Smoking gun? I've heard that said about dirt on Alabama's program plenty of times, but nothing ever comes of it."

"There's never been any dirt like this."

"Oh?"

"Yeah, watch this video Tre'vell forwarded me," Dixon said as he pulled out his phone and replayed the footage. It lasted just over a minute.

Once the video ended, Sanders stared at Dixon, mouth agape. "Does anybody else know about this?"

"I don't think so. If they knew I had it, I'd likely be dead now, too."

"What are you sayin'?"

"I'm sayin' this video is what got Tre'vell killed."

"You really think that?"

"Coverin' up a murder in Saint-Parran is far easier than tryin' to refute this video."

Sanders nodded and stroked his chin. "Hard to disagree with that."

"So, you think there's still a spot for me at Alabama?"

"Son, we'll name a building on campus after you if you give me that footage."

Dixon smiled. "Great. All you have to do is get Coach Raymond down here to agree to meet with me and guarantee me a spot on the team in writing."

"He can't do that."

"He will if he wants this footage. Bryant's not the only one I've got dirt on—just remember that."

Sanders scowled. "Let me call Coach Raymond and see what I can do."

"I'll look forward to hearing from you," Sanders said as he jammed his hands into his jacket pockets and walked toward the parking lot. His new Audi TT awaited him. And he didn't care who saw him. He didn't care what people wrote about him on Twitter either. He was sure he was going to play for the University of Alabama.

***

Hugh Sanders remained behind the field house several minutes after Dixon left. He didn't want to cause the young man any more trouble than he already had. *No teenager should get a red sports car and be subjected to anything but good ole-fashioned jealousy.* But Sanders had more important matters to address.

He walked to his truck and climbed in before hitting speed dial.

"What's going on now?" Alabama coach Dick Raymond said as he answered his phone.

"You're not going to believe what I just saw."

"Unless it's the second-coming of Herschel Walker or Bo Jackson, I don't want to hear about it."

"Oh, this is something you'll want to hear about."

"Why's that?"

"I just saw the reason why Tre'vell Baker and Dominique Dixon decided to renege on their commitment to Bryant University."

"You saw it?"

"Yeah, it's a video. It wouldn't be admissible in court, but the NCAA would take it."

"What do you mean?"

"It's something you have to see for yourself."

"Send it to me then."

Sanders took a deep breath. "It's not that simple. I don't

have a copy of it. And Dixon won't give me one unless you come down to visit him and guarantee him a scholarship."

"I can't guarantee him anything. He's the one who dragged his feet. We got our backup target in Dallas—and he's got a lot less baggage than Dixon."

"Maybe so, but Dixon's got something that will sink Bryant."

"Sink them?"

"Yeah, like the NCAA death penalty."

"What time should I be at the airfield in the morning?"

"Be there at six a.m. I'll take care of all the arrangements and have you back in Tuscaloosa by ten. Does that work for you?"

"I'll be ready at six."

Sanders hung up and texted Dixon details of the next morning's meeting.

"This just might be better than winning a championship," Sanders said to himself.

CHAPTER 23

FRANK JOHNSON STARED at his beer bottle and smiled. A sports anchor on the television at the end of the bar at Bons Temps reported the demise of high school superstar Dominique Dixon. Every college interested in Dixon withdrew their scholarship offer, according to anonymous sources, of course. The ever-watchful eye of the NCAA created a cottage industry for compliance officers at universities across the country, all employed to ensure that their school's coaches adhered to every recruiting guideline. It was the only way to shirk constant inquiries and probation threats from college athletics' governing body.

He felt a jolt to his arm and nearly spilled his beer. He turned around to see Phil Potter sliding into the seat next to him.

"What do you think about that?" Potter asked as he gestured toward the television. "That kid should've stayed in state and gone to LSU."

Johnson laughed. "Why? So he could finish second every season?"

Potter glared at Johnson but stopped once he caught the eye of the bartender so he could order a drink. Once the drink was ordered, he returned his gaze to Johnson.

"LSU still beat Bryant like a three-legged yard dog this year," Potter snipped. "Better than finishing near the bottom of the league every year."

"We're on the way up," snarled Johnson.

"It's the only way your sorry team can go."

Johnson buried his face in his hands. He'd set himself up for Potter's barb, one that stung because it was true. Despite all of Bryant's money, not much had been able to wrestle the balance of power away from Alabama. He finally looked up. "One day, it'll happen. You can count on it."

"Not if you scare away five-star recruits like Dixon and Baker."

Johnson rolled his eyes. "My school isn't the one that can't keep top talent in state. That's your school."

Potter didn't hesitate before he socked Johnson in the jaw, knocking him to the floor. Johnson stood up and bum-rushed Potter. The altercation lasted all of ten seconds before other patrons stepped in and broke up the fight.

The bouncer escorted the pair to the door and shoved them out by the back of their shirt collars.

"Sober up before you come back tomorrow, boys. And start actin' like grown ups."

Johnson touched the corner of his mouth with the fingers on his right hand. He checked his hand: blood. It wasn't much, but Potter got the better of him.

"So that's how it's gonna be?" Johnson asked.

"It is if you don't keep your big mouth shut," Potter grumbled.

"My big mouth is shut. It's yours that I'm worried about."

Potter walked away and then shot a look back at Johnson over his shoulder.

"Watch what you're doing, Potter," Johnson said. "This might not end well for you."

Potter turned back around and hoisted a middle-finger salute in to the air as he walked toward his truck.

"I've got pictures, you know," Johnson said.

Potter froze. He then spun around and marched back toward Johnson. "What do you mean you have pictures?"

"I mean, I have pictures. Don't even think about going off half-cocked on me. There are always consequences for your actions. And I'm here to ensure there won't be any consequences, provided you keep your mouth shut. Understand?"

Potter nodded and then walked away without saying another word.

"Everybody has secrets, Potter," Johnson said. "Especially you."

CHAPTER 24

CAL MOANED WHEN HIS ALARM went off at 3:30 a.m. Friday morning. Kelly groaned and whacked him with a pillow, urging him to move faster to turn off the alarm. Within the next thirty minutes, Cal took care of the essentials—including a short shower—and was on his way to the world's busiest airport for a 6 a.m. flight to New Orleans.

On Thursday night, Cal exhausted every idea he could think of to persuade Gatlin to let him return to New Orleans.

"A booster for hire is not an interesting story? Are you kidding me?" Cal protested to Gatlin the night before.

"It's not nearly as juicy as a story about a kid with a brand new red sports car that his uncle gave to him—the same uncle who works as a janitor at the school," Gatlin retorted.

Cal resigned himself to the fact that getting the story—and hopefully a book deal—required him to stretch the truth, if not ignore it altogether. Before he left the house, he pulled out a thermometer and shoved it next to a lamp. Then he jammed it in his mouth for a few seconds before memorizing the number on the digital display: 100.8. *Good enough for me.* He left a message on Gatlin's voicemail explaining that he took his temperature and it was 100.8 and he wouldn't be coming into the office. It was all to assuage his conscience that would only feel guilty until he uncovered what was really going on in Saint-Parran.

***

Dixon walked to the airfield to meet Hugh Sanders. With all the harsh attacks on social media, Dixon changed his mind about his brazen attitude the night before and decided a low-key profile was best for now. Driving his new red sports car to the airfield to meet the Alabama coach wouldn't do anything for his tarnished reputation.

Dixon arrived at 7:30, just in time to watch Sanders' jet touchdown on the tarmac and taxi toward his hangar.

"Good mornin', Dixon," Sanders said. "Did you bring the video?"

Dixon nodded.

"Good. Coach Raymond is looking forward to seeing it."

"Is he staying for our game tonight?"

"Unfortunately, he's got some things to attend to in Tuscaloosa later today, like getting ready to play Kentucky."

"He has to prepare for Kentucky?" Dixon asked.

"You have to prepare for everything if you want to succeed in life," Raymond said as he approached Dixon.

"Coach Raymond, it's nice to see you. Thanks for comin'," Dixon said.

"Oh, there wasn't much that was going to stop me once I heard what you had in your possession. I need to see it for myself. I'm sure you understand," Raymond said.

"I didn't know you coaches tattled on each other," Dixon said.

"We don't usually, but that's only when it pertains to cheatin'. What you're allegin' is a far more serious allegation that needs to be dealt with immediately by the powers that be. That is, if what's on that video is what you say it is."

Dixon nodded. "It's real. And it's the only way Tre'vell convinced me to pull our commitment. We knew it was big when it happened."

"So, let's see it," Raymond said.

Dixon pulled out his phone and began playing the video.

In the video, Baker was recording as he walked down the hall in the Bryant athletic offices. He took footage of jerseys and plaques of star Bryant players who had gone on to play in the NFL, the Bryant trophy case, the plaque outside Gerald Gardner's office. Baker became silent as he walked down the dimly lit hall. One of the doors was cracked and a beam of light escaped into the hallway.

Baker moved to the shadows and aimed the camera in the direction of the crack, through which he could see one of the assistant coaches.

"That's Harold Chambers," Raymond said as watched the footage. "That snake has lied about me more times than I can count to steal some recruits from me."

After a few moments, Chambers counted out ten $100 bills and handed them to one of the players. "I know it was hard to fumble that ball and cost you a touchdown, but I hope this makes up for it," Chambers said. "You went above and beyond the call of duty." The door then swung open and out walked Taylor Harmon, one of Bryant's best running backs. He shot Baker a glance before the camera shook and went fuzzy and then black after Baker shoved his phone into his pocket.

"They're point shavin'!" Raymond said. "Placing bets in

Vegas against the point spread and giving kick backs to the players. That's despicable. Who does that?"

"Bryant University," Sanders said. "Those low-life thugs have no morals whatsoever. If they can't pay their players from boosters, the coaches are bettin' against their own team and makin' sure they don't cover the spread."

"Son, you give me a copy of that video and I'll make sure you have a scholarship next year at Alabama," Raymond said to Dixon.

"Is that all? No other benefits?" Dixon asked.

"Take it or leave it. We're the University of Alabama. You might be able to peddle this to some other team around here and get a scholarship. But don't count on it after your social media fame yesterday. This is as good as it's goin' to get for you—it's as good as it gets for any kid who wants to play for the best football team in the country."

"Let me think about it," Dixon said.

"If I don't hear from you in the mornin', you can forget about it. You got more baggage than a bleached-blonde Tennessee tramp and I ain't got time to coddle you. So make up your mind and call me in the mornin'."

Raymond thanked Sanders for the usage of his plane and walked right back to it, jaunted up the steps and closed the door. Dixon hadn't even exited the airfield before the plane was airborne.

"Don't let this opportunity slip through your fingers," Sanders shouted at Dixon as he walked away. "It's not every day that the head coach of the University of Alabama flies down to meet you."

Dixon nodded and waved. He needed to think. If only Tre'vell were still here to tell him what to do, it would make his decision much easier.

CHAPTER 25

This time when Cal landed in the Crescent City, there was no Phil Potter to greet him. Cal was on his own this time—he preferred it that way. While Potter proved to be a useful guide, Cal felt he might have a better chance at uncovering what was going on if he went solo. He rented a Yukon so he wouldn't stand out and headed south.

By the time he drove into Saint-Parran, it was nearly ten a.m. He pulled into the Lagniappe Café. He needed to see Gertie.

"Back so soon?" Gertie asked Cal as he walked in the door.

"Who told you I left?" Cal asked.

"If this town were a head, it'd be nothin' but a giant mouth."

Cal smiled as he took a seat at the bar. "Just couldn't get enough of your coffee, Gertie."

"Now, that's a lie if I ever heard one." Gertie turned over a mug and filled it up. "If you really flew all the way back just for our coffee, it's on the house this mornin'."

"That's kind of you, but I'm here for another reason."

"Oh? And what might that be?" Gertie asked as she wiped the counter.

"I'm looking for this guy," Cal said as he dug his picture of Guy Lewis out of his pocket and showed it to Gertie. "Have you ever seen him in here?"

"Sure have. He was in here just the other day," she said as she inspected the picture. "Terrible tipper."

"You know much about him?"

"I know I've seen him in here on separate occasions wearin' an Alabama hat and an LSU cap."

"You sure about that?" Cal asked as he sipped his coffee.

"Honey, that's about as odd as seein' a two-headed alligator. There are some things that just ain't right. And when you see somethin' that ain't right, you don't ever forget it."

"Does he come down here often?"

"No, just every once in a while. I don't know much about him, but I don't like him. He gives me the creeps."

"And not much of a tip either."

"Yeah, you tend to not forget those folks."

"Thanks for your help, Gertie."

"My pleasure, Mr. Cal Murphy. You take care of yourself now."

Cal smiled and nodded before he tossed a five-dollar bill on the counter. If Gertie was going to remember him, it wasn't going to be because he was a lousy tipper.

***

Cal climbed into his Yukon before someone tapped on his window. It was Phil Potter. He motioned for Cal to roll down the window.

"Back already? And you didn't even call? Did you even think about how that would make me feel?" Potter asked.

Cal smiled. "You're a big boy, Potter. I figured you could

take it. Besides, we've got tight budgets these days. Haven't you heard that newspapers are a failing enterprise?"

"Seriously, why are you here?"

"There's still plenty to this story that I don't have yet." Cal winked at Potter. "See ya around."

Cal looked ahead as he rolled up the window. He cut his eyes over at Potter, who stood and stared at him. Then he said loud enough for Cal to hear through the window, "Be careful out there."

Cal didn't acknowledge Potter as he put the vehicle in reverse and backed out onto the main road. Potter served a useful purpose for the first couple of days, but Cal needed to take control of his investigation without watchful eyes and a gossiping mouth accompanying him.

On the radio, Cal struggled to find anything that eased his mind. A looming financial crisis for the U.S. government, the threat of war in the Middle East, a dive in the stock market. Not that any of those things directly affected Cal. But immersion in the dark side of humanity always made him search for some ray of light. He changed the station and didn't get what he was hoping for.

Hurricane Phyllis continues to strengthen in the Gulf of Mexico and is now a Category 2 hurricane with sustained winds of a hundred and five miles per hour. Right now, Phyllis is projected to make landfall late Saturday night. However, there's also a front sweeping in from the east that is going to bring a lot of rain with it this afternoon. Officials have issued flash-flood watches in several parishes along the coast, including Toulon Parish.

Cal needed to work fast if he was going to gather enough information for this story and escape town ahead of the storm.

After a ten-minute drive, Cal pulled up to Lanette

Baker's house. She and her two sons dashed between the house and her car, lugging boxes and bags. Lanette barely acknowledged Cal when he said hello.

"You guys trying to escape the storm?" Cal asked.

"There's always one brewin' down here," Lanette said as she walked toward the house. Then she stopped. "Well, don't just stand there, Cal. Come make yourself useful."

Cal followed her into the house and received the box she shoved into his arms.

"I'm afraid this isn't a great time to talk, unless you want to help," she said.

"I don't have a lot of questions, but I do have a few," Cal said.

"Fire away."

"Did you find anything of interest while you were cleaning out Tre'vell's room?"

"Like something that would make someone want to kill him?"

"Or anything that would help me get a better picture of who he was," Cal said as he followed Lanette outside.

"No and no. I already told you everything you need to know about Tre'vell."

Cal jammed the box into Lanette's trunk. "OK, I thought I would ask anyway. So, where are you headed again?"

"A long way from here," Lanette said as she turned toward the house again.

"Well, I'd love to send you a copy of this story once it's finished if you're interested—that is, if you have a forwarding address."

"Why don't give me your card, Cal, and I'll contact you once I'm settled."

Cal pulled out his wallet and dug out a business card for her. He watched the boys continue to work in silence. They avoided eye contact with him.

"Thank you so much for all your help. And again, I'm really sorry for your loss. I wish you all the best in your new venture."

Lanette then stopped. "Cal, can I ask you a favor?"

"Sure, what is it?"

"Just drop it. I don't want to keep reliving this nightmare. We buried my boy yesterday and I'd just as soon let him lie. You can write about what a wonderful young man he was but don't go tryin' to solve his murder. It's only gonna make things more difficult for us."

Cal nodded. He felt empathy for Lanette—but he couldn't shake the feeling that she was hiding something more than just where she was headed.

Lanette said good-bye and returned to the task of loading her car. Before heading back to his vehicle, Cal looked inside Lanette's car. A map rested on the front seat with a highlighted route from Saint-Parran to Huntsville, Alabama.

CHAPTER 26

BY NOON, THE SKY OPENED up and began dumping rain. Cal gritted his teeth as he opened the door to his truck and sprinted toward the door to the sheriff's office.

Sheriff Mouton stood next to the receptionist's desk as he looked over pages attached to a clipboard. He didn't look up as he spoke. "What brings you in here today, Mr. Murphy? Did you find the murder weapon or get a confession out of someone?"

"Good afternoon, Sheriff. I'm wrapping up my story and I had a few more questions to ask you."

"I don't know what I'd like to see leave town faster— you or this storm headin' our way."

"So, you don't mind answering my questions?"

"I make no promises, but proceed. I've gotta busy day ahead."

"Have there been any new developments in the homicide case of Tre'vell Baker?"

"Who said it was homicide?"

"Seriously? Getting shot accidentally from a long range is a common occurrence?"

"You don't live in the bayou. Bullets outnumber people down here a thousand to one. They can be thick as a hive of hornets at times." Sheriff Mouton exchanged the clipboard in his right hand for a cup of coffee.

"What has ballistics shown you about the gun that fired the bullet?"

"Ballistics? What do you think this is here? CSI? We have no need for them since we've determined it was an accidental shooting by an anonymous hunter."

"And Lanette Baker accepted that explanation?" Cal asked as he scratched down some notes.

"If I was worried about who might or might not accept the truth regarding our investigations, I'd never get any work down around here. Now, are you done yet? I've gotta get movin'."

"So you're saying that Lanette Baker was fine with your conclusion?"

"You're not going to stop, are you?" Sheriff Mouton asked as he slammed his fist down on the receptionist's desk. "If you must know, I spoke with Ms. Baker and she seemed satisfied with our findings. Not that she cares too much since she's itchin' to get outta town."

Cal scribbled down a few more notes and then looked up. "Thank you for your time, Sheriff Mouton."

"Watch yourself out there, Mr. Murphy. There's a storm a comin'—and you ain't seen anything like it. I suggest you get back to Atlanta real soon."

Cal nodded and turned to exit the office. He tucked his notepad under his jacket and sprinted back to his SUV.

Once inside and safe from the rain, he flipped through several pages. Cal held everyone in suspicion—Hugh Sanders, Frank Johnson, Sheriff Mouton. Even Lanette Baker acted jumpy when he questioned her. What really happened that afternoon to Baker seemed destined to remain a mystery if the guarded members of Saint-Parran had their way.

***

Cal decided to grab some lunch at Bons Temps. When he pulled into the parking lot, he couldn't find a spot. He settled to park alongside the road like several other patrons had done. Inside, Cal fought his way through the throng of people enjoying an afternoon of drinking and storytelling. Every table he passed contained at least one person using the word "storm" in it. *War stories for bayou residents.*

"What'll ya have?" asked the bartender as Cal sat down.

"What's the special?"

"Boudin and beer. It's a tradition to serve it the day before a storm," the bartender said as he slid a menu in front of Cal.

"Why's that?"

"One year a long time ago, we served boudin and beer as the special and the hurricane changed course and left us alone."

"So this wards off hurricanes?" Cal asked as he glanced at the menu.

"You kiddin' me? This is bayou country where we leave a welcome mat out for monster storms. We're all crazy for livin' here, that's for sure."

"But when it's calm, it's a beautiful place."

"Don't let still water fool ya. It ain't ever calm in the bayou."

Cal smiled and drummed his fingers on the bar. "I think I'll take the black and bayou burger, fries and a glass of water."

"Good second choice," the bartender said as he jotted

down Cal's order. "My name's Moose if you need anything else."

"Thanks, Moose. What I need more than a burger is to find out what everybody in this town is hiding."

"This place buries secrets before washin' them out to sea. If people around here want to keep it hidden, you ain't ever gonna find out," Moose said. He toweled dry several beer mugs.

"I'm beginning to think you're right."

"Any secret in particular troublin' you?"

"Yeah, the one about Tre'vell Baker's death."

"Hmm. That's a difficult one for sure. I haven't heard anything about it."

"I'm just having a hard time believing a random bullet fell from the sky and killed him after he decided to withdraw his commitment from Bryant."

Moose put his elbows on the bar and leaned in close to Cal. "Be careful with those boys from Alabama," Moose said as he nodded toward Hugh Sanders sitting alone at a corner table. "They don't take too kindly to being stiffed."

"So, you think somebody from Alabama is responsible for Tre'vell Baker's death?"

"All I'm sayin' is that once Baker and Dixon reneged, I heard that somebody from Alabama approached Baker about going there. But he turned them down and said he was going to Texas A&M instead."

"I haven't heard anything like that."

"You only hear what people want you to hear, Mr. —?"

"Cal. Cal Murphy. I write for *The Atlanta Journal-Constitution*."

Moose put his hand over his mouth in a playful manner. "Perhaps I've already said too much—and there was a good reason why people weren't telling you anything of the sort. But what do I know? I'm just the bartender."

"But why would someone affiliated with Alabama want to kill Baker?"

"Jealousy? Teach him a lesson? Maybe the reason why he wouldn't go to Bryant was he saw some NCAA rules being broken and he wouldn't rat on 'em. You just never know."

"I just find that hard to believe."

"The bayou will make a believer out of you if you stay down here long enough. If you ever think you've seen it all, somethin' will change. You'll swear again that you've seen it all—until the very next day when somethin' crazier happens."

Moose left for a few moments to fill some drink orders. Cal grabbed a handful of peanuts in a bowl on the bar. He cracked them open and thought about Alabama's motivation. Cal remained deep in thought until he felt a firm hand on his right upper arm jar him back to reality.

"What in the world are you doin' here?" asked the man. Cal spun around to see Hugh Sanders. "I'd heard you already high-tailed it back to Atlanta."

"The food's too good to be gone too long," Cal quipped.

"So's the fishin'," Sanders added. "Seriously, why are you back?"

"And here I was wondering why you haven't left yet to get out of here ahead of Hurricane Phyllis."

"I'm not going to miss Saint-Parran's playoff game tonight. We've got plenty of time to escape this storm."

"That's exactly why I'm back. I want to help paint the scene for readers when I write this story about Baker and Dixon."

"It's still a shame about that kid," Sanders said as he

shook his head. "He was flat out amazin'."

"But not a future star at Alabama?" Cal asked, as he watched to see how measured Sanders' response would be.

"Unfortunately, I don't think he was ever going to go to Alabama. Several other colleges had caught his eye by the time the word got out that he wasn't going to Bryant."

"And Alabama wasn't in the mix?"

"Maybe. But if Alabama was, it wasn't the frontrunner. If you're lucky enough to have a chance to go to Alabama but decide to go elsewhere, you might as well not go at all," Sanders said as he motioned for Moose to refill his shot glass. "The choice is really simple. You can play for championships your whole college career—or you can try to beat Alabama."

Sanders slammed back the shot and took in a deep breath. "Hopefully, Dixon won't make the same mistake."

"Mistake?"

"Any time you spurn Alabama, it's a mistake, Cal. Or haven't you been livin' in the south long enough to know the foundational tenets of college football. Alabama is king and everybody else just wants to be Alabama."

Cal smiled and shook his head.

"You disagree?" Sanders asked.

"No, I just think it's funny that you think so highly of Alabama. It's not like your team wins the title every year— even when you get all the best recruits. Need I remind you of Mike Shula. It wasn't that long ago—"

"Enough. That's a name best left unsaid, the real scarlet A on our program—and not the same A that's worn proudly by our fans."

"So even you have to admit that Alabama isn't always a perennial power?" Cal asked as Moose slid a plate of food in front of him.

Sanders shook his head. He motioned to Moose for another shot. "I don't have to admit anything except that no college football team has more national championships than Alabama."

"What about Princeton? I read they have twenty-eight."

"You can't always believe what you read, Cal. You ought to know as well as anyone."

"The next thing I'm going to write in the paper is who killed Tre'vell Baker and why."

"Be careful, Cal. You might not be able to handle such a story."

"Don't you worry about me, Mr. Sanders. I'll be just fine."

"Stay dry," Sanders said before he threw back another shot and slammed it down on the bar. He sneered at Cal before walking away.

Moose moved over to talk to Cal. "What'd you do to get his goat?"

"I guess I made fun of Alabama," Cal said as he sopped up some ketchup with his fries.

"Better be glad that was only his sixth shot of the afternoon."

CHAPTER 27

AN HOUR BEFORE KICKOFF, Frank Johnson entered the Saint-Parran High press box overlooking the field. The thrum of the rain on the tin roof drowned out all other sounds. Due to the deluge, not a soul stood on the field. As he stared at the lights beaming onto the field, the rain descended sideways.

"And the real storm isn't even here yet," Johnson said to the scorekeeper, who only grunted and failed to look up as he pored over the rosters for the game. Johnson walked through the main press box area and into one of the empty coaches' booths. He sat down and began dialing a number on his cell phone.

"Everything's set," Johnson said. "It's only a matter of time before we end this thing once and for all."

"Good work, Johnson. I appreciate you staying on top of this matter for us. You know how important this is."

"I sure do, Coach Gardner. You won't be disappointed."

Johnson hung up and stared at the night sky. He felt a twinge of regret about what he was about to do. *It's for the greater good.*

He then put a pair of ear buds in his ears and opened up an app on his phone. The app enabled him to listen in on another phone. He had to break a few laws to hack his way into the other phone and place the malicious malware there, but he justified it. *That fool always leaves his phone on the table when he goes to the bathroom. It's his fault. Besides, it's for the greater good.*

He increased the volume in his ear buds and listened to the conversation.

"Hi, Coach Raymond. It's Hugh Sanders here."

Johnson increased the volume again and smiled.

***

Hugh Sanders sloshed through the muddy parking lot. His Orvis jacket shielded him from the driving rain. It would've kept him warm and dry in a blizzard, too. He sported a pair of Orvis fly-fishing waders and a pair of boots handmade in France. No foul weather would spoil what the night held in store for him. With or without Dominique Dixon going to Alabama, it was going to be a triumphant night.

He pulled out his cell phone and jammed it tight to his ear beneath his hood.

"Hi, Coach Raymond. It's Hugh Sanders here."

"Any news on Dixon? I wanted to send one of our defensive coaches down there tonight, but we couldn't make it work."

"No news yet on either front. Hopefully, Dixon will give us a copy of the footage from Baker's cell phone and we can sink those bastards from Bryant."

"I prefer to serve punishment on the field. Besides, sometimes revenge isn't what it's always about."

"Then what is it about?"

"It's about leverage."

Sanders stopped walking and squinted at the lights as the rain poured down. "Are you suggesting we don't leak this video to the press?"

"Like the great philosopher George Strait once said, 'You've got to have an ace in the hole'."

"You're the boss. I'll take care of things over here tonight and call you once it's finished."

"You're a good man, Hugh. Roll Tide."

"Roll Tide." Sanders hung up and shoved his phone back into his pocket. He then made his way over to the field house.

When he opened the door, Saint-Parran High coach Hal Holloway greeted him.

"Now, fellas, here's a man who knows how to handle the elements," Holloway said.

"Better to be prepared than be miserable," Sanders said. "Besides, I wouldn't miss this game for anything. Got to root you guys on tonight."

Sanders smiled and winked at Dixon.

"Coach Holloway, I don't want to intrude too much, but I was wonderin' if Dominique had decided where he's attendin' school next year," Sanders said as he shuffled into the locker room before settling on a spot to stand against the wall.

"If he has, he hasn't told me," Holloway said. Then he turned toward his star cornerback, "Dixon, get over here."

Dixon jumped up and walked over toward Holloway and Sanders.

"Yes, Coach?" Dixon asked.

"Have you made up your mind about where you're goin' to school next year? This fella here is mighty interested," Holloway said.

Dixon flashed a wry smile. "Come talk to me after the game."

"Will do," Sanders said before he thanked the coach and exited the building.

CHAPTER 28

LANETTE BAKER KICKED her car's back left tire and cursed. Her car, jammed with every worthwhile belonging, had picked this moment to blow out a tire. In the time it took her to inspect the tire, the rain drenched her. Not a stitch of dry clothing left.

"What are we gonna do?" Nikko asked his mother once she returned to the car.

Lanette beat on the steering wheel for a few seconds and cursed some more.

"Why does this always happen to me?" she cried aloud. Then she began wailing, unleashing the floodgates of emotion that until this moment had remained pent up. "I can't catch a break for nothin'. I can't even escape this town when I'm tryin' to escape it. It's like a vicious monster that won't let me go." Then she wailed some more.

Jarvis joined his mother and started sobbing. "I miss him," Jarvis stammered.

"Me, too, baby. Me, too." She helped Jarvis climb into the front seat and held him in her lap while they cried.

After a few minutes, she pulled out her cell phone to make a call and get some help. The battery was dead. She pounded on the steering wheel again.

"What's wrong now, mom?" Nikko asked again.

"Battery's dead."

"I'll go get help if you want me to," Nikko said as he grabbed the door handle and awaited her blessing to leave.

She stared out the windshield spattered with raindrops. In the distance, she could see the glow of the Saint-Parran High stadium lights. Coach Holloway had asked her to come to the game as the players wanted to pay tribute to Tre'vell and honor her as well. But she couldn't bear the thought of being around the very thing that reminded her of the essence of her son. Not now. Not so soon. She wanted to put this nightmare behind her instead of dredging it up a day after she buried her eldest son.

Lanette cracked the window and could hear a man over the public address system announcing the starting lineups. She then rolled up the window.

"Let's just stay here until the rain dies down." She remained transfixed in the direction of the stadium.

"But it's never gonna stop," Nikko protested.

"It always passes, son—just before another takes its place."

***

Cal stamped his feet once he entered the Saint-Parran press box. Two sports writers occupied the only seats made available for the press. Nicholas Turner, the local sports editor who also covered education and business for *The Toulon Times*, occupied one of the seats, though Cal wondered if Turner wouldn't be more comfortable in two seats. Next to him was Luke Alexander, a correspondent for the *Times-Picayune* out of New Orleans. Both glanced at Cal when he walked in but neither was about to give up their prized piece of real estate.

Cal asked the announcer if he had any extra rosters. He didn't, but Cal took a picture with his phone of the only one he had so he could follow some of the star players.

Early in the game West St. John took a 6-0 lead when one of the defensive lineman recovered a fumble at the 2-yard line to set up an easy score. But then Saint-Parran found its rhythm.

A long run by the team's leading rusher along with an extra point gave Saint-Parran a 7-6 lead. Dixon later intercepted a pass and returned it 40 yards for a touchdown to give his team a 14-6 lead. Then just before halftime, Coach Holloway sent Dixon in to play receiver and he caught a screen pass that he turned into a 55-yard touchdown play. Saint-Parran held a commanding 21-6 halftime lead.

"What do you think?" the announcer asked Cal as he turned around.

"He's more impressive in person," Cal answered.

"Better than anything you've seen in Atlanta, I guaran-dang-tee ya," Turner chirped.

"Better than anyone I've covered there, that's for sure," Cal said. He wanted to justify Turner's pride. The truth was Cal had yet to cover a high school football game since he moved to Atlanta.

As the players exited the field, one of them collapsed. The players huddled around him and a buzz fell over the stadium followed by an eerie hush.

"Who's down?" the announcer asked.

Turner picked up his binoculars and peered onto the field. "It's hard to tell. Everybody's so close around him." Some of the players shifted around as two paramedics rushed in. "Oh, wait. It looks like Dixon. Yes, that's him all right."

Cal tore out of the press box and raced down the steps.

He jumped the fence and hustled over to the players huddled around him. Cal passed Dixon's mother, who was also sprinting toward the pack.

"What happened?" Cal asked Coach Holloway, who stood a few feet behind the paramedics.

"We don't know. He just suddenly collapsed."

"Has he ever done this before?"

"Not at practice or any other time that I'm aware of."

Cal paced around as he watched the paramedics work. Dixon's mother knelt down next to him and held his hand. The paramedics helped him up before giving him some oxygen. They then transferred him to a stretcher.

"He's gonna be all right," one of the paramedics said. "It looks like he's had a reflux episode."

Cal fought his way through several players standing next to the stretcher, where Dixon sat up.

"Back up. He needs his space," the other paramedic said as he shooed away Cal and the other players.

Dixon then locked eyes with Cal and extended his pinky and index fingers on his right hand, locking down the other fingers with his thumb. Then he flashed the numbers "three" and "four" before nodding at Cal.

What does that mean? Does Dixon like to rock? Is he a Texas Longhorn fan? And then is that thirty-four or three and four?

Cal knew Dixon was trying to tell him something, but what? For a kid immersed in the world of college football, that symbol was notorious with Texas' fans "Hook 'em Horns" symbol. But what did that have to do with anything? To Cal's knowledge, Dixon never seriously considered Texas as a school he wanted to play for.

He raced back to the press box to report the good news that Dixon would be fine. He passed the information along to the announcer who assured the crowd that Dixon was not seriously injured or ill, though his status for the second half was unknown.

With his mission completed, Cal slipped into the coaches' box and began to think about what Dixon was trying to say. He then entered "Longhorns 34" into the search engine on his phone's browser. The first few entries to pop up were related to former Texas star running back Ricky Williams. Below them appeared an entry containing a box score from several weeks ago: Bryant Huskies 43, Texas Longhorns 34.

Cal read through the details of the game but nothing clicked with him right away. It seemed like it was innocuous. Maybe he needed to look at some of the other entries. Then Cal stopped. In a small box at the top of the story was the Las Vegas betting line: Bryant -10. Bryant was favored by ten points. Then Cal noticed a line in the story about Bryant's star running back who rushed for 150 yards and three touchdowns and one fumble. Cal scrolled over to the play-by-play chart of the game. It detailed every player involved on each play, including down and distance. Cal searched all the way until he found what he was looking for late in the fourth quarter.

With two minutes remaining, Bryant's running back fumbled on the 5-yard line. Usually, the play-by-play chart would mention what defensive player forced the fumble, but there wasn't one. The absence of a defender's name meant the running back fumbled on his own. *The ball just slipped out of his hand?* First, he checked the weather for the game. At kickoff, it was 68 degrees and sunny. Then he checked the player's season stats. It was his only fumble of the season through ten games.

Was Dixon trying to tell me what this looks like—that Bryant was point shaving? Could this be what Tre'vell Baker found out?

Cal shoved his phone back into his pocket and exited the press box. He needed to talk to Dixon again.

CHAPTER 29

FRANK JOHNSON snuck into the Saint-Parran field house. The kerfuffle he helped create by providing an extra spicy pre-game meal for the players triggered a reflux episode in Dixon. It was something one of the Bryant coaches mentioned offhand to him shortly after Dixon's visit to the school. Following one of the evening meals, Dixon had a reflux episode that gave everyone a scare.

Johnson did his research. He tasted several varieties before settling on Burpee's supersteak tomatoes, which were so acidic they curled his toes. He gave the caterer a bushel of the tomatoes with a special request that the sauce be homemade according to the details of a special family recipe. The truth is there was nothing special about it. It was extra spicy and comprised of his choice tomatoes—all designed to elicit a reflux response in Dixon. It worked like he planned.

Once inside the field house, Johnson wasted no time. He located Dixon's locker and walked straight toward it. He scavenged around until he found what he was looking for: Dixon's phone.

Johnson began searching through his email and found one from Tre'vell Baker that included a video attachment.

He opened it up and watched a conversation between one of the Bryant coaches and players that clearly indicated they were point shaving.

If this video ever fell into the wrong hands … Johnson shuddered and sent the video to himself. He deleted both the copy from Baker and the copy he'd just sent to himself in the outbox. He used a handkerchief to wipe off all his prints before his final point of business. Searching for a blunt object, Johnson picked up a helmet and smashed the phone with it. He slid the mangled device back into Dixon's bag and exited through the back of the field house. He peered around the corner to see if anyone would see him leaving.

He muttered a few curse words under his breath. Cal Murphy was headed straight for the field house.

***

The Saint-Parran High marching band waded onto the field and began a routine that included Michael Jackson's *Thriller*. Cal winced as he heard the dissonance trying to emulate musical genius. As he made his way down the grandstand steps, he contorted his face at the moment a loud off-key note echoed through the stadium. It was a look that apparently caught the eye of an elderly gentleman.

Leaning against the fence, the man turned to face Cal and began speaking.

"It's times like this that I bet you wish you had a pair of these," the man said, gesturing to his hearing aid devices snug behind each ear.

Cal smiled and nodded as he kept walking. Once he exited the stands, he dodged a group of elementary-aged boys engrossed in their own game of touch football just beyond the stands. He quickened his pace as he walked headlong into a gusting wind.

Cal's phone buzzed. It was Gatlin.

"Hello," Cal said.

"Sick, huh?" Gatlin asked.

"Look, I can explain."

"I don't want any explanations, Cal. I just want you to do what I tell you to do. I let my reporters have long leashes to explore stories, but when I say that's enough, that's enough. I've been in journalism longer than you've been alive and I know when a story isn't materializing. So unless you want to vanish with that story, I suggest you get back here on the next plane or else don't come back at all."

"But, you don't understand—"

"I don't want to understand. I just want you back here. Got it?"

Cal reached the edge of the field house and leaned against the outer wall. There was just enough of an eave to shield him from the rain falling directly down. It did little for the rain whipped sideways by the rhythmic blasts of wind.

"Listen to me, Gatlin! I think I know what got Baker killed."

"OK, I'm listening."

Cal lowered his voice. "I think they found out that Bryant was point shaving during their visit."

"Do you have any proof before you make such an accusation?"

"No, not yet. But I think I may be able to get some."

"Great. You can get some from Atlanta. I want you back here tomorrow to cover the Hawks. And maybe if you somehow get a story out your wild adventure down there, I'll forgive you and won't make you cover another one. Got it?"

"But Gatlin—"

"We're done talking about this. Call me once you're on the road. I don't want you trying to pull anything over on me this time."

"This is big, Gatlin. I—"

"I don't wanna hear it. Get back now if you value your job, Cal."

Gatlin hung up. Cal sighed and gently rapped his head against the exterior field house wall. *This is too good to pass up. Screw it. I'm gonna stay here until I find out what's going on.*

Cal's phone rang again.

"Kelly?" Cal answered.

"When are you coming back?" Kelly asked.

"I don't know. When I have feel like I have enough to write my story. Probably a day or two."

"I suggest you get back as soon as you can."

"Why's that?"

"Gatlin called here looking for you and I slipped up and told him you weren't here—"

"That explains it."

"Explains what?"

"I just got a call from him and he chewed me out, demanding that I come back to Atlanta right away. But I'm getting close to this story. I want to see where it leads."

"No, Cal. You can't do that. You can't lose your job. If you don't get this story and that book deal, it's not the end of the world. We can survive without a surgery, but not without your job."

"But, Kelly—"

"I'm sorry, Cal. I wasn't thinking when I told him that. My mind's been a bit loopy lately. But you've gotta come back. You know it wouldn't look good to get fired because you were moonlighting for a publisher in pursuit of a book deal—all without your editor's approval."

Cal sighed and said nothing.

"You get back here as soon as possible," Kelly said.

"OK, OK. I'll call you later."

Cal hung up. He needed to think. He needed to talk to Dixon.

***

Around the corner, Frank Johnson felt his chest tightening. He hated dirty work. It's why he went to college in the first place.

"You see those guys wearing orange vests and digging that ditch?" his father would ask as they were driving by road construction sites. "That's gonna be you if you don't get a good college education. Stay in school, son. It'll pay dividends for you way down the road—and I guarantee you that you'll never have to dig ditches for a living."

Johnson didn't mind hard work as long as it didn't require getting his hands dirty. But his college degree couldn't help him avoid the dirty work now before him.

CHAPTER 30

INSIDE THE SAINT-PARRAN field house, Dominique Dixon returned to collect his bag. One of the paramedics waited for him at the door.

"Are you all right, 'Nique?" one of the players asked.

"Yeah, I'll be fine," Dixon said.

"Are you going to be able to play any more tonight?" another player asked.

"I don't know. Ask him," Dixon said as he gestured toward the paramedic.

Observing the interaction between Dixon and his teammates, the paramedic nodded. "There's a very good possibility he'll be able to come back. We just want to run a few more tests on him before releasing him."

Coach Holloway rubbed Dixon's head as he walked by. "Hurry up and get back out there. We need you."

Dixon smiled and nodded at his coach before exiting the field house and walking toward the ambulance. His mother waited by the ambulance as well.

"He's going to be fine," one of the paramedics said. "We just need to do a few more tests, Mrs. Dixon."

Dixon followed the paramedics and climbed inside the ambulance. He sat on a small table as the paramedics prepared to inspect him before giving their final approval.

While Dixon waited, he dug through his bag, searching for his phone.

"What the—" Dixon said as he felt a mangled mess of plastic parts at the bottom of his bag. He scooped it up and pulled it out. For a few moments, he stared at the smashed pieces of his cell phone before he started crying.

"It's OK, kid," one of the paramedics said. "It's just a cell phone. They're a lot easier to replace than you."

Dixon stopped crying and grimaced as one of the paramedics poked and prodded him. He now knew why Tre'vell Baker was dead—and it had nothing to do with a stray bullet from a hunter's rifle. Now someone was on to him, too.

***

Cal rapped on the ambulance doors parked next to the field house. Dixon looked startled as he motioned for Cal to come in. Cal climbed in despite the immediate protest from the paramedics.

"You can't be in here," one of the paramedics said.

"It's cool. Just leave him alone," Dixon said.

"No! I'm sorry, sir, but you must leave now."

Dixon stood up. "Fine. We'll take it outside."

Cal jumped out of the ambulance with Dixon behind him. Dixon's mother grabbed Dixon's face with both her hands. "Are you OK, son? What's wrong?"

Dixon shrugged her off. "I'm fine, mom. But I need some privacy to talk to Mr. Murphy here."

Cal stepped over to the side to let the drama unfold.

"Anything you say to him, you can say to me," she said.

"No, I can't. And it's for your own good. Trust me," Dixon said.

She relented and moved away to give them privacy. Cal noticed her still leaning in with her ear to try to hear what they were saying.

"Were you trying to tell me what I think you were trying to tell me?" Cal whispered.

"What do you think I was trying to tell you?" Dixon whispered back.

"That Bryant was point-shaving?"

Dixon nodded.

"So why are you telling me this now?" Cal asked.

"Because I think someone is on to me. I think someone made me ill on purpose and when I got back to the field house, I found my cell phone all smashed up."

"Why would they do that?"

"Because Tre'vell recorded one of the coaches giving money to the running back. This is what I wanted to show you before you cancelled our meeting yesterday. Tre'vell recorded this through a crack in one of the coaches' doors and nobody saw us. But I told Alabama about the tape. I don't think somebody from Alabama would destroy it as they were really anxious about getting their hands on it. All I can figure is that somebody else obviously knows it exists."

"I think I might know who might be doing this."

"Well, stay away from them—and don't write anything about this. I'm pretty sure that's what got Tre'vell killed," Dixon said.

"And that's exactly why I have to write about it," Cal said. He patted Dixon on the shoulder. "Get back out there and finish these guys off. I've got to get back to Atlanta, but I'm going to be back."

"Be careful, Mr. Murphy—and please leave my name out of it."

Cal nodded. He doubted he could comply with Dixon's request, but it didn't matter now. He might not ever write the story if Gatlin got his way.

***

From the stands, Hugh Sanders looked through his binoculars at a discussion between Cal Murphy and Dominique Dixon taking place near the ambulance.

I wonder what that's all about.

He watched as Cal spun and walked toward the parking lot at a swift pace. Just as he was putting his binoculars down, he noticed another familiar person emerge from the shadows. It was Frank Johnson.

CHAPTER 31

CAL CLIMBED INTO HIS YUKON and checked his watch. It was 8:15. If he hustled, he could make the 10:45 p.m. flight from New Orleans to Atlanta. He buckled up and called the Delta reservation line as he began maneuvering out of the parking lot. He drove over a handful of potholes brimming with rainwater and splashed his way onward until he reached the road.

In a matter of moments he had changed his flight. Now all he needed to do was pray that there were no nasty wrecks that would hold him up on the roads.

He began to mentally go over everything he knew about the story. Baker and Dixon reneging on their commitment to Bryant. The strange circumstances surrounding Baker's death. Someone trying to frame Alabama for illegal recruiting. Dixon telling Alabama about the tape. In the cutthroat world of recruiting, Cal couldn't rule out any school for wanting to take down Alabama. Auburn, Tennessee, LSU, Florida, Bryant—they all loathed the empire in Tuscaloosa and would dance a jig on Alabama's grave. Experience taught him not to jump to conclusions.

Before Cal had the chance to mentally sort through the motives of each party involved, he noticed the flashing hazard lights of a car parked on the shoulder of the road. As he passed it, he looked to see what the problem was. He saw a flat tire right away before he fully recognized the car— it was Lanette Baker's.

He slowed down and looked at his watch. He could change a flat tire in ten minutes. He'd timed himself before. If he hurried he'd still have time to make it to the New Orleans airport with a few minutes to spare. He pulled over in front of the car to see if he could help.

Cal held the map from the rental car agency over his head as he jogged over to the driver's side window and tapped on it. "Lanette, are you all right?" he asked.

The windshield wiper blades swished back and forth for a few moments before she moved. She rolled the window down just enough for her voice to escape through a crack. "Does it look like I'm all right?"

"Well, do you want me to help you change that flat tire?"

"The tow truck is on his way."

"You don't need a tow truck. I can fix that for you. Let me help you."

Cal stopped his pleading when a large truck pulled up behind Lanette. The bright lights and the persistent rain made it difficult to tell who it was. He leaned back down toward Lanette's window. "Looks like the cavalry's here. Best of luck to you."

He turned and walked away. Above the steady sound of the rain pounding the pavement, Cal heard quickening footsteps on the pavement. Before he could turn around to see what was happening, a burlap sack was shoved over his head while his hands were held down. He wrestled to pull the sack off, but his assailant zip-tied his hands behind his back and shoved him toward his truck.

"Who is this? Why are you doing this to me? You can't just abduct me like this!"

No response.

"Come on, man. I'm begging you, whoever you are. Don't do this. Let's talk about whatever it is that's bothering you."

Still no response.

"This isn't how we do things where I come from. Let's have a conversation. Do you want me to help you get some message out to the media? I can do that. Whatever you want, I can help you with it."

"Don't struggle so much. We're on the same team. All I want is you." The voice was resounding, clear, powerful. Cal recognized it immediately.

It was Hugh Sanders.

***

"Mom, we can't just sit here and do nothing," Nikko said to Lanette. "They're kidnapping Mr. Murphy."

"He can take care of himself," she said.

"No, he can't. That guy just threw him into the back of his pickup truck."

"Maybe Mr. Murphy deserves it. Justice in the bayou doesn't always look the same as it does everywhere else. Besides, you don't know what he did, son."

"It doesn't matter—Mr. Murphy has been tryin' to help us and now you won't help him?"

"Mr. Murphy has been tryin' to help himself at our expense. Don't confuse his desire to write some story about Tre'vell with his caring about us."

"But he stopped and tried to help us in the pouring rain. He wasn't going to get a story out of that."

Lanette rolled her eyes. "You're as relentless as your older brother. How in the world did I get a family of do-gooders?" She shook her head and looked ahead at the road. "Where is that tow truck? It should've been here a long time ago."

"Mom, you didn't call one," Nikko said.

"Cyrus Wilhelm cruises up and down the road at least once an hour in his truck huntin' for business. He'll eventually find us. Just you wait and see."

***

Hugh Sanders watched Cal writhing about in the back of his pickup truck as he turned off the main road and onto a dirt road riddled with potholes. He slowed to ten miles per hour as he crept along. With the keenness of a hawk, Sanders scanned the road for a turnoff well hidden by shrubs and bushes. *Bingo!*

Sanders put his truck in park and ran over to move the shrubs and bushes that were loosely laid on the ground to cover the roadway. He drove through the makeshift gate and continued on until he reached a small clearing at the water's edge.

CHAPTER 32

THE TRUCK FINALLY STOPPED and so did the wind and rain. Aside from his own breathing against the burlap sack, Cal could hear a cacophony of bullfrogs and other swamp wildlife. Had the situation been any different, he might have relished this moment in nature. Instead, Hugh Sanders shocked him by abducting and transporting him to this remote location.

He strained to hear anything else. After a few moments, he could hear the muffled voice of Sanders. *What is going on?*

Cal heard the truck door open and a rhythmic high-pitched sound that warned Sanders his keys were still in the ignition. Cal sat up as he heard the door slammed shut followed by the sloshing of footsteps.

Without warning, Sanders yanked the burlap sack off Cal's head.

"What do you think you're doing?" Cal demanded as he squirmed from a sitting position.

Sanders leaned on the truck. He appeared calm and in control. "Now, calm down, Cal. It's not what it seems."

"It seems like you've lost your mind! Now untie me and take me back to my truck. I've got a flight to catch tonight."

"There's been a change of plans. You won't be leaving

here any time soon."

"This is absurd. You ought to be ashamed of yourself."

Sanders rocked back and forth as he glared at Cal. "Ashamed of myself? For what? Doin' the right thing? Sometimes doin' the right thing takes more courage than doin' the wrong thing, if you know what I mean."

"I don't know what you mean and I don't know what you're talking about. Please take me back right now."

Sanders shook his head. "No can do, amigo. I've got something on the agenda for us that you might actually appreciate."

"The only thing I'll appreciate is you taking me back to my truck."

"Now, Cal, you just need to relax and trust me. We both want the same thing here."

"And what might that be?"

"The truth."

Cal paused for a moment as he stared at Sanders. His shook his head and looked downward as he spoke. "This isn't how you get the truth."

Sanders reached into the truck bed and pulled out a large flashlight. He shined it into a nearby bank. Two alligators on the shore dodged the light by sliding into the water.

"Well, it's how we're gonna get it tonight at Devil's Point. Now, you just keep your mouth shut, let me do all the talkin'. And who knows? You might just get out of here alive."

Cal sighed. "Can you at least untie me instead of treating me like some criminal? I'm not going anywhere and nobody is looking for me."

Sanders grunted and walked toward the truck. He dug a sharp hunting knife out of his coat pocket and cut Cal loose. "No funny business. You understand?" Sanders said as he backed away and shined his flashlight into the water where three alligators had now gathered.

Cal nodded. There was nothing funny about the text message he furiously wrote while Sanders scanned the swamp.

***

The moment Frank Johnson received a call from Hugh Sanders he marched right out of the stadium and toward his truck. Saint-Parran had taken a commanding 34-12 lead on West St. John early in the fourth quarter—and now Johnson had more important business at hand.

He climbed into his truck and slammed his fist on the steering wheel before turning the ignition. He paused a moment before launching into a tirade that included both cursing and punching his dashboard. "How did this happen? I *know* that was the only copy of that video left!"

Johnson roared down the highway, riding the centerline as he jammed his foot on the accelerator pedal. He recognized Lanette Baker's car as he flew past it.

"That ungrateful wench! Her stupid son screwed everything up!"

Johnson activated the speaker function on his phone and called Bryant coach Gerald Gardner.

"What's the good news, Frank?" Gardner said as he answered.

"There's no good news right now, Coach."

"That's not what I wanna hear."

"I know, but I'm going to rectify the situation shortly. I'll let you know when it's done."

"Anything I should be concerned about?"

"There's another copy of the video."

Gardner remained silent.

"Coach? Are you still there?"

Nothing.

"Coach?"

"You better find that tape, Frank. You know what that will mean for all of us if it leaks out. We're finished—all of us!"

Gardner hung up.

Johnson could feel his blood pressure rising as he sped down the highway.

"I'm gonna tear Sanders apart!"

Lost in his rage, Johnson failed to see the oncoming car in his path until it was almost too late. He swerved at the last moment to avoid a collision before slowing down. Johnson looked in his rearview mirror and saw the other car sliding off the side of the road and into a ditch.

He stomped again on the gas and kept driving.

"You're a dead man, Sanders!"

CHAPTER 33

WITH THE RAIN STOPPED and still no sign of Cyrus Wilhelm and his tow truck, Lanette Baker decided to walk for help. She didn't get more than a quarter of a mile down the road before a truck pulled off on the shoulder in front of her. It was Phil Potter.

"Lanette Baker, what are you doin' out here? You havin' car trouble?" he asked as he hopped out of his truck, which remained running.

"Yeah, Phil. I blew out a tire and my phone was dead. Of all the nights not to see Cyrus Wilhelm drive up and down this road at least once."

"Cyrus has got steadier work tonight," Potter said. "I heard on my scanner there was a big accident on the other side of the parish."

"Well, that explains it."

"I also heard about an erratic driver around here. You haven't seen anything like that, have you?"

"No. Why you askin'?"

"Oh, nothing really. I was watchin' the game from my truck while half listenin' to the scanner and the ball game on the radio when I saw Frank Johnson dart into the parkin' lot like a bat outta hell. Just wondered if it might be him."

"You're ever the snoop," Lanette said.

"Hop in and I'll drive you back to your car and fix your flat."

Lanette climbed into his cab and rode with him back to her car. Outside the car, Nikko was unloading the trunk to get to the spare tire. Potter parked and he and Lanette both got out and walked toward her decrepit vehicle.

"I can do this, mom," Nikko said. She threw her hands up in the air and rolled her eyes.

"You got some mighty fine helpers there," Potter said as he pointed at Nikko. "You might even have yourself another football star. Maybe he'll even go to LSU."

Lanette paused before she answered. "I'd prefer if Nikko or Jarvis took up art or music instead. I'm done with football."

Potter arrived at the back of her car and began to help Nikko unload. "You can't keep a good strong kid like Nikko here away from the football field. It's where he was born to be. Don't try to force a square peg into a round hole," Potter said.

"We'll see."

Nikko and Potter continued unloading until they finally reached the spare tire and pulled it out. Potter worked the jack until it lifted the car sufficiently off the ground to replace the tire.

"Say, Nikko, you didn't happen to see anybody go racin' down this road a little while ago, did ya?" Potter asked as he put on the spare.

"I sure did," Nikko said. "Maybe fifteen minutes ago some big truck came roarin' past here."

"Did it look like Frank Johnson's truck?"

"I think so. I've seen him at my house enough the past

few months that I oughta know what it looks like."

"Did you see where it went?"

"If it turned off anywhere, I didn't see. He was flyin'."

Potter tightened the nuts on the tire and lowered the car with the jack.

His phone buzzed with a message. He looked at it and shoved it back in his pocket.

911 devils point cal

"You should be all set," Potter said as he helped Nikko refill the trunk. "I've gotta run." Half of the Baker's belongings still sat alongside the road.

"Thanks, Phil," Lanette said. "Oh, and one more thing."

"What's that?"

"Can I borrow your phone real quick like? I need to make a call before we leave."

"I've really gotta get goin'."

"It'll only take a second."

Potter relented. "Make it quick," he said as he handed her the phone before walking around to the back to help Nikko finish packing.

Less than a minute passed before Lanette walked around to the back of her car and handed the phone back to Potter. She thanked him again, but he didn't respond, taking the phone as if it were a baton in a relay race. Before Nikko could put another box in the trunk, Potter had already rumbled away.

***

Cal drummed his fingers on the side of Hugh Sanders' truck. With Sanders tight-lipped about his plan, Cal decided to employ his interviewing skills and see if he might be able to sneak something out of his captor.

"How many grandkids you got?" Cal asked.

"Three," Sanders said.

"My son, Bear, has two boys that are four and two."

"What about your other grandchild?"

Sanders paused for a moment and sighed. "Crimson has a six-year-old daughter," he answered.

"Why the hesitation?"

"It's not my proudest moment as a father."

"I'm just doing all I can just to become a father."

"Well, you'll screw up, don't worry. I just hope it's not as much as I did, especially with Crimson." Sanders flashed his light back toward the water where four alligators were now visible.

"What'd you do to Crimson?" Cal asked. He was still in the truck bed but moved toward the tailgate before sitting on it.

"Long story."

"I've got nowhere to be unless you change that."

"She started dating a local football star behind my back. I wasn't havin' any of it once I caught them sleeping together. But it was too late. She was already pregnant."

"A pregnant teen daughter? That sounds tough."

"Yeah, then to spite me, the guy went to play at Bryant. He could've gone anywhere, but I know he went there just to get at me. But he never saw the field. Flunked out after two semesters and was in prison six months later." Sanders then spit on the ground.

"How are things now between you and your daughter?"

"Terrible. I don't even see her any more. I haven't seen my granddaughter in over four years."

"Sorry to hear that."

"Yeah, it's enough regret for a lifetime," Sanders said. He paused when it sounded like something was walking through the woods. He shined his light on a doe scampering through the forest. "That's why I'm not livin' with regret any more."

"So that's why I'm here?" Cal asked.

"Exactly. I'm gonna make sure not another kid from around here goes and gets their life screwed up at that school."

"And that's all?"

"Well, if they don't kill ya, I hope you can write a heck-uva story and take down those bastards."

"What do you mean, *if they don't kill me*? What do you intend on doing with me?"

"You'll see."

Cal surveyed the area and wondered if he could escape. He knew he could outrun Sanders, but where would he go? How long would he last before he stumbled into the swamp? Or before Sanders caught up with him? It was risky for sure, but Cal's curiosity kept him planted on the back of Sanders' tailgate.

"So, you're saying I'm bait?" Cal asked.

"Yep."

"What's this really all about?"

"I think you know," Sanders said as he flicked his flash-light on and shined it on the water. Five alligators now gath-ered near the shore's edge.

"That's a grand assumption since I was just trying to help a woman who'd just lost her son fix her tire before you grabbed me. Before that I was on my way out of town so my boss wouldn't fire me for sneaking back down here against his wishes."

"I think you know more than you're lettin' on."

"I wish you could read my mind and tell me what I know—cause I don't know what you're talking about."

Sanders walked near the truck and pulled out a phone. "Just watch this and you'll figure it out." Sanders pushed play on the phone and a video started.

It was Tre'vell Baker's footage of Bryant University running back Taylor Harmon taking money for point shaving.

Cal sat stunned once the video finished. It was journalism gold. He could almost see his name on another plaque for his national award-winning story—and on the cover of a new book. "Do you think this is why Baker got killed?"

"Maybe. If this video ever goes public, it'll ruin the careers—and lives—of several coaches and players, if not the entire Bryant program all together."

"Something tells me you wouldn't mind seeing that."

"While there's definitely some truth to that, I've learned that there's always something more you can get out of a situation like this."

"Such as?"

"You'll see."

"You think I won't write about this now?"

"Not if I give you a better story—and you've got no evidence to prove this."

"What makes you think I wouldn't write it anyway and cite myself as a deep source?"

"Don't think I don't know who you are, Mr. Cal Murphy," Sanders said. He shined the flashlight into the water. All five alligators remained motionless in the water. "You're a journalist with a bright future ahead of you, but need I remind you that any attempt to cross me would mean you'd be taking on the entire University of Alabama. And if that doesn't frighten you, I'm afraid you haven't been in the south long enough to know fried okra from chitlins."

"So, what's this better story?"

"If you make it out of here alive, I'll tell you how many NCAA rules Florida broke to get their latest Heisman Trophy winner—and how many laws he broke that disappeared off his record before they signed him."

Cal couldn't get past Sanders' first clause. "Stop saying, *if I make it out of here alive.* This cryptic talk is ridiculous. Quit jerking me around. Tell me what the plan is."

"Just keep quiet and do as you're told. You'll be fine soon enough if things go as intended."

Sanders shined his light back onto the water. Six sets of alligator eyes now peered over the dark waters in Devil's Point.

Cal seethed as he pondered how to escape. Nothing ever went like it was supposed to go.

CHAPTER 34

FIVE MINUTES LATER, the headlights of another vehicle shone on the main road. It looked like a truck to Cal, but he couldn't be sure what kind or whose it was. But Sanders recognized the visitor.

"OK, get ready," Sanders said. "Just be quiet and leave the talking up to me."

Sanders meandered toward the oncoming truck, waving the flashlight at the driver. The truck then turned off the main road and rambled over the bumpy terrain until it stopped a few yards short of Sanders, who stood a few feet in front of the back of his truck. Cal remained motionless on the tailgate of Sanders' truck as he hoped this nightmare would end soon.

The driver turned off the engine but left the headlights on. He climbed out of the vehicle, his feet landing with a thud in the marshy terrain. Sanders shined a light on the man. It was Frank Johnson.

"I've got half a mind to feed you to those gators," Johnson yelled at Sanders as he climbed out of his truck and slammed the door.

"I doubt it'd be the first time you did somethin' like that," Sanders said. He edged closer toward Johnson as he shined his flashlight onto the pistol in his hand.

"What is this? A set up?" Johnson said as he gestured toward Sanders' gun.

"That's your department, pal. I'm just playing my part."

"What's that supposed to mean?"

"I think you know, but I didn't invite you out here to get into a tit-for-tat. You're here to discuss the transfer of some evidence." Sanders held up a phone. "It seems like there's more than one copy of video footage showing some indiscretions by the Bryant coaching staff. And I thought maybe we could make a deal."

"What kind of deal are you talkin' about?"

"I'm talkin' about a gentleman's agreement between me and you, Alabama and Bryant."

"Go on."

"I'll give you the last remaining copy in circulation of Taylor Harmon taking money from one of your coaches in exchange for the promise that Bryant abandon all its recruiting efforts in lower Louisiana. Anything from New Orleans on down across the entire state is off limits. I'll be holding one copy in a secure location in case this agreement is ever breached."

Cal sat stunned. This isn't how he suspected the confrontation to go between Sanders and Johnson. *A recruiting cease and desist?* A kid may have lost his life over this video and now it's being traded for something like this? Something didn't seem right.

Johnson grunted and paused before he spoke. "Say I get Coach Gardner to agree to this, we've already got a verbal commitment from Deshawn Hightower, the top overall quarterback in the country out of Edna Karr High. We can't just ditch him."

"You will if you want this footage. I didn't say it'd be

easy, but it's a nice alternative to having the NCAA sniffing around your program, much less the feds. There's always more dirty laundry to be found, and you can bet they'll find it all."

Johnson nodded and took a deep breath. He put his hands on his hips. "Looks like you win, except for one thing."

"What's that?"

"What to do about him," Johnson said as he pointed at Cal.

"He's part of the deal," Sanders answered. "You can do whatever you want with him or make your own deal with him. He's all yours now."

Cal panicked. He made a quick move to jump out of the truck bed before he heard a noise that froze him in his tracks.

Click.

"I wouldn't do that if I were you," Johnson said.

Cal turned around slowly to see Johnson aiming a gun at him. He then looked at Sanders. "You lyin', back-stabbin', son of a—"

"Now, now, Mr. Murphy. No need to be callin' anybody any names. We're out here on business, just like you were. Diggin' through other people's trash can leave you with a stench that's difficult to wash off. And you stink to high heaven, son."

"What about that story you were gonna give me if I kept my mouth shut?" Cal asked Sanders.

"Perhaps Frank has one for ya. And as long as it's not about Alabama, he's well within his means to strike any deal he wants with you regardin' such information."

Cal looked at Johnson, who now wore a mischievous grin. "Well?"

"Well what? I don't have any plans to be striking any deals with the likes of you. I've got something else in mind."

Cal surveyed his options, none of which yielded great odds for survival. Run and hope Johnson is a terrible shot and a lousy tracker, all while counting on being able to evade swamp critters and search parties in a dangerous and unfamiliar environment. Or promise never to print a word of the story, likely enabling him to keep his life but possibly costing him his job as well as dashing Kelly's dreams. Then there was Johnson's mysterious plan—a plan he seemed intent on going through with. Staying alive seemed preferable, which kept Cal from darting off into the swamp for the time being.

"And what exactly do you have in mind?" Cal asked Johnson.

Before Johnson could answer, Sanders butted in. "Ssshhh. You hear that?" he asked in a whisper.

All the men froze and collectively held their breaths in an attempt to hone in on the sound Sanders claimed to hear. After a few seconds, the cause of the sound became evident. It was a truck rambling along the road as its headlights bounced up and down on the surrounding woods.

"Can you tell who that is?" Johnson asked in a whisper.

Sanders shook his head. "Not yet."

But Cal had a hunch his text had worked. Then as the truck turned off the main road and started coming toward them, Cal knew who it was by the sound of the engine.

It was Phil Potter.

CHAPTER 35

DOMINIQUE DIXON LINGERED in the field house following Saint-Parran's victory over West St. John. He craved the big stage and wanted to close out his high school career with a state championship in the Superdome in New Orleans. He then wanted to experience the roar of a hundred thousand fans celebrating one of his great plays at the collegiate level.

He looked at his phone, smashed to pieces. If he were ever going to hear such a sound, it wouldn't be from the fans of those cheats at Bryant. Nor would it be at Alabama. *They had to be the ones who did this. Who else knew about what I had on my phone.* But there was far more on his mind than what college to attend or whether or not to leak damning evidence about Bryant University's football program.

"You all right?" Coach Holloway asked Dixon, the lone player in the locker room.

"I think so, Coach."

"Tryin' to decide where to play?"

"Yeah. I've just learned a lot in the recruiting process."

"Such as?"

"Such as I can't trust anybody except myself."

"Not everybody's like that," Coach Holloway said as he sat down next to Dixon.

"Everybody I've met is," Dixon said. He snapped and unsnapped the chinstrap on his helmet several times. "It's all about how I fit into their plans. *Their* plans. Nobody has once asked me what I want to do, what my dreams are all about. It's all about how I can help them accomplish theirs."

"Well, what do you want?"

"I want to escape this place and see the world. I've lived in the bayou my whole life and it feels like an island, even a prison at times."

"What about playing in the NFL? Is that a dream of yours?"

"Of course, it is. But I've started to think differently about life these last few days."

"Because of what happened to Tre'vell?"

"Exactly. I thought life was all about football, family and fun. But I know there's more to it than that," Dixon said as tears started to roll down his face. "I miss Tre'vell and I want to live the right way, the way that he lived always lookin' out for others first."

"That'd be a great way to honor his memory," Coach Holloway said as he patted Dixon on the back.

Dixon wiped his face clean of tears and looked up at his coach. "Thanks for listening."

"Any time. So, what's it gonna be? Alabama? Bryant?"

"Neither, I'm gonna play at Clemson. They didn't ditch me after all the stuff that happened yesterday. I actually got a call from one of the coaches telling me they weren't giving up on me despite the media reports about what happened."

"You told Coach Raymond that yet? I heard he flew down here just to meet you earlier this week."

"He's one of those people I don't trust," Dixon said.

"Besides I always wanted to go to Clemson, but it was

too far away for Tre'vell. He wanted to stay closer to home. But now that he's gone, I wanna do what's best for me— and maybe one day I'll be half the man Tre'vell was."

CHAPTER 36

PHIL POTTER PARKED HIS TRUCK and got out. He lumbered toward the two vehicles already parked near the edge of Devil's Point. A light cast on him by one of the men forced him to shield his eyes.

"You guys throw a party and didn't invite me?" Potter asked.

Sanders shined the line near Potter's feet once he spoke. "Don't you crazy Cajuns know how to mind your own business?"

"It's my business to know," Potter snapped as he kept walking toward them.

"Not tonight it isn't," Johnson said.

"Oh, Frank, you're here too," Potter said. "My two favorite infidels from the state of Alabama. Why don't you boys just get on back to where you belong? I have a feeling you're up to no good out here."

"How'd you know to look for us here?" Johnson asked.

"Anytime Frank Johnson leaves abruptly in the middle of a football game, there has to be somethin' going on that's worth seeing. So, I followed you."

"I don't believe you," Johnson said. "We've been out here for a while."

"There are only so many places to go in Toulon Parish if you want to take care of business," Potter said.

"What makes you think we're out here having a business discussion?" Sanders asked.

"There's a guy sittin' in the back of your pickup, Hugh, and he's been awfully quiet," Potter said. "Maybe we should ask him. Who is that anyway?"

"He's none of your concern," Johnson said. "Now, I suggest you turn around, head back to your truck, and forget that you ever saw us here."

Potter heard the click of a pistol and froze. "OK, OK. I don't want any trouble."

"If you didn't want any trouble, you should've never followed me out here—if that's even true," Johnson snipped.

"Maybe it wasn't my brightest move, but—what are you guys doin' out here anyway? Decidin' Dixon's fate? Castin' lots to see who will get him?"

"Dixon's free to go wherever he wants to go," Sanders said, "as long as it's not Bryant University. I'd hate for the young man to make such a mistake."

"Is that what you said about Tre'vell Baker?" Johnson asked Sanders. "If he doesn't go to Alabama, he doesn't go anywhere?"

"In case you haven't figured it out yet, killin' ain't my style," Sanders said. "But Potter on the other hand …" Sanders let his words hang in the air as if to create a simple inference.

Johnson aimed his light at Potter, who threw his hands in the air. Potter panicked. He started to sprint for his truck. In less than five steps, Johnson fired a warning shot into the air.

"The next one is going to hit you in the back and kill you," Johnson said. "I wanna hear this."

***

Cal remained quiet. He wanted to hear this, too. Ever since he saw the note found in Tre'vell Baker's backpack, Cal had a nagging feeling he'd seen the handwriting somewhere before. He just couldn't remember where. Was it at Lanette Baker's house? The Dixon's house? The bar? The restaurant? He couldn't recall where he'd seen it—until now.

"Turn around and come back here right now," Johnson said.

Potter complied as he kept his hands extended in the air. "I don't want any trouble," he said.

"Neither do we," Johnson said. "We just want the truth. Did you murder Tre'vell Baker?"

"Murder is such a harsh word," Potter said. "I never meant to kill anybody."

Cal's mouth dropped. He couldn't remain silent any more. "What do you mean you never meant to kill anybody?"

"Oh, so that's you over there, Cal," Potter said. "I was beginnin' to wonder if you were pullin' my leg."

Sanders shined his light in Cal's eyes. "Did you call him out here?"

"Maybe," Cal answered. "But I'm not your concern now, remember?" Then to Potter. "So, tell us what happened."

"Everyone around here was mad about him announcin' that he was going somewhere else, even his mama," Potter said. "One day I was in Café Lagniappe and I ran into Lanette Baker. She asked me to talk some sense into Tre'vell. So I tried, but he didn't want to hear any of it."

"So you wrote him a note?" Cal asked.

"Yeah, I wrote him a note just to try and scare him a

little bit, maybe make him reconsider what he was doin'. Then I went too far. I had been drinking down at Bons Temps when I left and passed his place. I saw him and Jarvis out fishin' and decided that I'd just shoot a little warning shot over his head to shake him up." Potter paused for a moment. "I never meant to hurt him, honest."

"You shot him in the back of the head and you were just trying to scare him? How do you explain that?" Johnson demanded.

"I—I don't know. I just aimed in his general direction, but I didn't think there was any chance it'd actually hit him," Potter said.

"Dropped him dead right in front of his little brother, too," Sanders added. "You're a worthless coward."

From the rage building in Sanders and Johnson, Cal sensed where this confrontation was headed—and it wasn't a good place. Potter must have sensed the same thing as he spun around and dashed toward his truck. He made it inside before Johnson fired a shot that blew out Potter's front left tire. Sanders shined the light on Potter, who put both of his hands in the air in surrender.

"Get back here right now," Johnson said. "And do it slowly. Keep those hands where I can see them. I wouldn't want this gun to accidentally go off."

Potter complied with the demands and kept his hands in the air once he climbed out of the vehicle.

Meanwhile, Cal thought this might be his best opportunity to run. With Sanders and Johnson preoccupied by another nemesis, Cal figured it might be his best chance to make it out alive.

Cal slid over the side of the truck and into the muck. With the ground damp and muddy, he treaded lightly to avoid making a suction noise that would attract attention. As he moved through the woods, he heard more raised voices and shouting before a few punches were thrown. Cal made it about forty yards away before he heard another commotion, this time caused by Potter's mouth.

"What happened to Cal?" Potter asked. It put the beating on hold as Sanders began scouring the woods with his light. Cal froze. To run would be to give up his only advantage in the moment. If he stayed hidden long enough, they would have to decide between him and Potter—and he was betting that they'd choose Potter. It was better odds than sitting in the truck waiting for whatever punishment Johnson had cooked up for him. If it was anything like Potter just received, Cal wanted no part of it. He eased closer to the ground and shielded himself from plain view by crouching behind a fallen tree nearby.

"You ever play Russian roulette, Cal?" Johnson shouted into the woods. "Well, we're gonna play Bayou roulette. I'm gonna shoot into the woods somewhere and I may hit you and I may not. Or I could always let Potter here shoot at you. He'd try to miss but he'd probably blow a hole in your head." Johnson then guffawed over his last statement.

Cal failed to see the humor in it. Nothing was funny about his situation. He remained frozen, flummoxed over the best route to take. Before he could decide, Johnson fired his gun.

"Cal! Come out, come out, wherever you are," Johnson cried as Sanders waved the flashlight throughout the woods.

Another round. Cal kept track. Four shots had been fired so far. He knew Johnson only had two more if that was his Glock 42 he'd bragged about.

"Cal! We can do this all night," Johnson said.

Another shot.

Cal prepared to run the instant he heard the next one echo into the night.

The sixth shot.

Cal didn't wait around to hear Johnson torment him. The codger was likely fiddling around for another clip, if he even brought another one.

"There he is!" Sanders shouted as he kept his flashlight trained on Cal.

Cal scampered through the trees and brambles, branches and limbs slowing his progress and scratching his face. It felt like an endless maze with no exit. *Where is the road? Where is some dry ground?* Cal found none. Instead, his toe found a fallen tree that sent him sprawling face first into the mire. He scrambled to get up before another warning shot ripped through the night.

"I can see you," Johnson said. "If you make another run for it, you'll be betting against the fact that I didn't bring another clip. It's not a bet you should take."

Cal raised his hands in the air and turned around.

"Get back over here now," Johnson demanded.

As Cal began to walk, he felt a sharp pain in his ankle. He hobbled back toward Devil's Point confident that he twisted his ankle. If he was going to escape now, it would require something more ingenious than a dash through the woods.

Johnson directed Cal next to Potter, who stood a few feet away from the water's edge. "Tie 'em up, Hugh," Johnson said.

"I'm not sure I wanna be a part of this," Sanders said.

"Now you have a crisis of conscience? Please. Tie 'em up or you can join them too," Johnson snipped.

Sanders wandered over to his truck and grabbed some duct tape and the burlap sack he'd used earlier with Cal. He gave his flashlight to Johnson, who shined it on the two prisoners. Sanders tied both Cal and Potter's hands behind their backs while he apologized.

"I never meant for it to end up like this, Cal. Honest," Sanders said.

"Spare me," Cal said. "You're starting to sound like Potter."

"Shut up! All of you!" Johnson said. Then to Cal, "I promise to make this quick for you." Without a warning, he shot Cal in his left leg.

Searing pain washed over Cal's lower extremities; blood spouted from the wound and soaked his pants. Before Cal could figure out what was going on, Sanders ran toward him and jammed the burlap sack over Cal's head, turned him around and kicked him in the back with his foot, forcing him into the water.

Cal sank into the swamp. He held his breath as he kicked around to locate the bottom. In a matter of seconds, he felt another big splash next to him. He figured it was Potter. The additional person struggling in the water created a sensation of turbulence. Cal found his footing and tried to stand upright. Though Cal couldn't see anything, he suspected he was just tall enough to keep his mouth and nose above the waterline, though with Potter splashing about next to him, he couldn't be certain.

As Cal bobbed up and down, he tried to make it out of the water. He heard Johnson and Sanders shouting about something, but he didn't know what. Then as he sensed the bottom begin to slope upward, Cal couldn't move. He felt more searing pain as something sharp clamped onto his leg and pulled him back toward the water.

Gators!

CHAPTER 37

JIM GATLIN TAPPED HIS PENCIL on his desk and checked his watch. *Why haven't I heard from Cal? Weren't my instructions to call me clear enough?* If Gatlin were a coach, he'd be considered a player's coach, someone who is friendly with his staff and treats them like equals. It was times like these that he regretted having such a chummy disposition. They always felt like they could walk all over him.

One of the staff sportswriters walked into Gatlin's office. "Everything OK in here, chief?"

Gatlin grumbled and shooed the reporter away. Then he flung some papers across the room and let out a string of expletives. "Why can't anyone do what I tell them to do?" he yelled.

He picked up his cell phone and began dialing Cal's number. "I'm going to teach that insubordinate punk a lesson," he muttered to himself as Cal's phone began to ring.

Five rings and no answer. The call went to voicemail.

He ended the call without leaving a message.

"Ahhhh!" he said.

He picked his phone back up and dialed Kelly to see if she'd heard from her husband.

"Hello?" Kelly answered.

"Kelly. Gatlin here. I'm looking for Cal. Have you heard from him?"

"No, I haven't. I spoke with him about an hour ago and told him he better get home quick. Why? Is something the matter?"

"Yeah, I'm pissed. He was supposed to call me once he got on the road and I haven't heard from him and can't get him on the phone."

"Maybe he doesn't have cell coverage. He's in the bayou, you know."

"Don't remind me. But if you hear from him, you tell him to give me a call right away."

"Will do. And can you do the same for me?"

"Sure thing." Gatlin hung up and banged his fists on his desk. *I'm gonna kill him—after I fire him!*

CHAPTER 38

FRANK JOHNSON SLIPPED THE FLASK out of his pants pockets and took a swig as he watched Cal and Potter squirm for their lives while the half-dozen alligators closed in on their prey. His first venture into corporal punishment and torture invigorated him. His stomach usually churned over such blood sport, but not tonight. Tonight was about maintaining honor for his favorite college football team.

"You're aren't going to just leave them there are you?" Sanders asked. "I'm sure they're convinced you're crazy enough to come after them now."

A smug grin spread across Johnson's face. "If I pull them out now, they'll think I'm weak."

"Come on, Frank. This is crazy. I didn't think you'd kill anybody over this."

"You mean you wouldn't do the same thing for Alabama if the roles were reversed?"

"Alabama would never pay players to shave points, so I can't fathom your hypothetical question."

Johnson seethed over Sanders' comment. "Oh, pardon me, the great and mighty Alabama never would do anything like this. They're so perfect and holy and all that is right in college football. We must all bow down and kiss Bear

Bryant's houndstooth hat. All hail the perfect angels from Tuscaloosa."

"Now, calm down. I never said anything like that," Sanders said. "I'm just sayin' that Alabama doesn't need to shave points to pay players."

"So, they do pay players? You probably give them all free cars, don't ya?"

"Don't put words in my mouth."

Johnson ambled toward Sanders and poked him in the chest with his index finger. "You're not denying it."

"Back off, Frank. And get those guys out of there before they get hurt."

The splashing and struggling in the water intensified. Johnson shined the flashlight onto the water and counted the alligator eyes. He could only see five sets of eyes—and one body.

"Where's Cal Murphy?" Sanders asked.

"I don't know," Johnson replied.

"Gimme that." Sanders snatched the flashlight from Johnson's hands and began to comb the water with the light in search of Cal. "I don't see him anywhere."

The thrashing died down for a moment before a big splash scattered water everywhere. Cal emerged from the water and let out a scream. "Somebody help me!"

Johnson remained unconcerned with the events playing out before him in the water. But when he heard a door slam behind him, he grew very concerned. He spun around to see a dark figure walking toward him. Johnson fumbled with his light until he trained it on the man.

"What are you fellas doing out here?" the man asked.

It was Sheriff Mouton.

***

Cal couldn't shake the alligator off his leg. He came up for air and wasted it on a cry for help through the drenched sack before the alligator yanked him back into the water. With the water saturating the loosely fitting tape on his hands, Cal broke them free. He instinctively ripped the bag off his head and then shoved on the alligator's snout to loosen his grip. It didn't work.

Think, Cal. Think.

It wasn't easy to think of anything creative in the moment. Primal fear dominated his thoughts. Hope began to fade as he winced from the pain in his leg, which he was all but certain was now broken.

How can I inflict the most pain to make this beast stop?

As Cal wrestled, he thought. He had nothing to smack the alligator on the snout, something he'd seen once on the Discovery channel. He couldn't punch him underwater hard enough to induce him to let go. Then it hit him.

The eyes!

Desperate to take another breath, Cal focused all his energies on reaching near his foot to feel the alligator's snout until he reached its eyes. He then jammed his thumbs into the alligator's eyes. Immediately, the alligator released him.

Cal frantically swam toward the small shoreline. He glanced behind him to see another alligator trailing him. Cal beat the water with every ounce of strength he had left. He had to rely on his arms as his legs were worthless when it came to creating propulsion through the water. Though the alligator had only dragged him about thirty feet from land, Cal thought he'd never reach it. He feared the alligator would grab him again at any moment.

Bang! Bang! Bang!

Cal reached the land and scrambled to his feet, hopping and stumbling toward higher ground. He clambered into the bed of Sanders' truck and turned around to look at the scene by the water's edge. Cal watched the alligator twist in the water after getting shot.

Sheriff Mouton trained his rifle on the water as Sanders waved a flashlight back and forth. Cal only counted five alligators, which seemed to be still for the moment. He noticed Potter had also escaped the water with no apparent injuries.

With everyone content that the alligators weren't coming ashore, Sheriff Mouton turned to face Cal.

"Somebody better start talkin'—and fast," Sheriff Mouton said as he waved his flashlight at the group.

Sanders chimed in first. Cal surmised it was in an effort to create the initial picture Sheriff Mouton would have and somehow help him avoid any accusations of wrongdoing. Cal was going to make sure that story didn't stick.

"Cal and I came out here to make a little transaction with Frank over some information he wanted," Sanders said. "Then Frank got a little erratic and tied these fellas up and tried to feed them to the alligators. He threatened to do the same to me if I didn't help him."

"Is that true, Frank?" Sheriff Mouton asked.

Johnson shielded his eyes from the glare of Sheriff Mouton's flashlight. "Not exactly. We threw them into the water, but it was Sanders who forced me to help him."

"That's a lie and you know it!" Sanders shouted.

The interrogation erupted into a free-for-all shouting match between Sanders and Johnson. Potter jumped in and began yelling at both of them with his own interpretation of the evening's events.

Sheriff Mouton squelched the argument by firing his rifle into the air. "Silence! I've had enough of these shenanigans for tonight. You're all coming back to the sheriff's office with me and we're gonna sort this out."

"Like hell I am," Johnson said as he started running.

Sheriff Mouton started cursing and fired a warning shot into the air. It didn't make Johnson pause. He tore through the woods like he was sprinting for the end zone.

"Go get in the truck," Sheriff Mouton said to the remaining men. "There are some blankets in there to dry yourselves off with and a first aid kit to dress that wound. Sanders, Potter—one of you fix up Cal. I'll be back soon. This shouldn't take long."

CHAPTER 39

FRANK JOHNSON SWIPED at his face with the back of his hand. The sweat beading up and rolling into his eyes burned. So did his chest as he panted for breath.

They think they can pin this on me. I'm not going to jail because of some Alabama lowlife's lies.

He'd almost convinced himself that the tale he'd spun for Sheriff Mouton was true. He would never try to feed two men to a pack of hungry alligators. Not him. That was what Alabama fans did. They poisoned trees. They desecrated stadiums. They shot each other when they weren't angry enough about losing to a rival. But that wasn't him.

He stopped to catch his breath and listen for anyone following him. The faint crunches of leaves and snapping of twigs echoed through the woods. He had to keep running.

After several minutes, he stumbled across one of the dirt roads that wound through the bayou and to some of the better fishing spots in the area. But he couldn't stay there long. Sheriff Mouton would surely apprehend him if he stayed in the open. He dashed across the road and kept running through the woods, using the road as a guide. If he recalled correctly, Johnson suspected he would come to a main road soon.

As Johnson ran, he reflected on how he got to this point,

running through the woods in the middle of the night like a criminal. *Just stop and turn around. Everything will be all right.* Johnson's conscience nagged at him, but it couldn't overpower the feeling that he was being lied to. The truth was he was going to jail unless he could get back to the main road, find a way to his jet and escape. Just fly to Mexico and blend in. Sell the airplane and live off the cash for a while. Or fly farther south after a few days and vanish for good. Those decisions weighed on his mind, but they could wait. He needed to get to the airfield first.

Several minutes later with his hunch proven right, Johnson staggered onto the main highway. Rain started to fall again, creating a slick film on the road's surface. It wouldn't be long before someone came along.

***

Gertie sat in her car and counted her tips before turning her car's ignition. Eight dollars in tips. Between the football game and the threat of another storm, Café Lagniappe spent more money on keeping coffee warm than it made. She sighed as she turned on her windshield wipers and put her car in reverse.

As she eased down the road, her mind drifted toward Lanette Baker. No matter how bad things had been for Gertie lately, she didn't have to endure the heartbreak Lanette had. Yet in some ways she envied Lanette. She wouldn't mind packing up and just moving out of town. Maybe things would be different if she could start over with a fresh slate. But there was something about the bayou. It gripped her soul in strange ways. Her desire to leave clashed with her desire to stay. And no matter how long she pondered, dreamed and thought about leaving, she always stayed. Leaving the bayou meant missing out on the unexpected. She thought about her paltry tip haul and let her mind churn over the idea of leaving before she would ultimately decide against it. It was a futile exercise, but one she often embarked upon. But this time it came to a halt with the screeching sound of her brakes.

Gertie's wipers worked furiously to clear the rain off her windshield, but it was plain to her what stood in the roadway ahead: a man waving a gun. It was Frank Johnson.

***

Out of breath, Sheriff Mouton arrived back at Devil's Point several minutes later.

"I lost him," he said as he climbed into his truck. He turned the ignition and the engine roared to life.

"What happened?" Cal asked. He fidgeted with the dress

"I followed him out to the road but before I could catch him, he flagged a driver down and was gone." Sheriff Mouton stomped on the gas.

Sanders leaned forward from his backseat position in the cab. "I know where he's going. You've gotta hurry."

"Yeah, there's only way he could escape the bayou—and that's by air," Sheriff Mouton said. "If he thinks I'm going to let him just fly outta here like that, I know tree stumps with higher IQs than him."

Sheriff Mouton turned onto the main road and stomped on the gas. Cal reached over and buckled his seat belt.

"First time on a bayou manhunt?" Sheriff Mouton asked.

"What gave it away?" Cal said.

"Relax, son. This is my specialty. It makes me happier than a tornado in a trailer park. We're gonna nail this bastard, just you wait."

CHAPTER 40

GERTIE TRIED TO KEEP her eyes on the road instead of the gun Frank Johnson aimed at her. If only she'd left town ahead of the storm. She needed every dime she could scrounge up, but her tips tonight weren't worth this. No amount was.

"Why are your hands shaking so much?" Johnson asked. "I'm not gonna hurt you."

"Then why are you pointin' a gun at me?" she replied.

"Insurance. I just want to make sure you don't do anything stupid." He tapped the passenger side dash. "Let's go. Faster."

She drove as instructed, silent for a minute.

"You don't have to do this, you know?" Gertie said. "Whatever it is, I'm sure there's a better way out."

"You don't know what I did."

"It can't be that bad."

"I tried to kill a man. Two men, actually."

"But you didn't, did you?" She glanced over at Johnson, who stared down at his gun.

He shook his head. "I wanted to. But now I've become like the very people I detest."

"If there's one thing I've learned in this life, Mr. Johnson, it's that bitterness and hatred will eat a hole right through ya—and you're always more like your enemies than ya think. That's why hatin' never does anybody any good."

"You might be right, but it's too late now."

"It's never too late to stop hatin'."

Johnson remained quiet for several minutes. "Turn here."

Gertie turned into the entrance to the Saint-Parran airfield and put her car in park. The gate was shut and required an access code for entry.

"Get outta here, Gertie. You don't want to be around to see this." He waved her off with his gun.

She didn't breathe for several seconds as she drove away. She watched him punch in a code on the access panel and the gate swung open. Gertie exhaled.

"Thank you, Lord, for keepin' me safe," she muttered under her breath.

She jammed her foot on the accelerator. She didn't want to be anywhere near the airfield when the sheriff arrived.

CHAPTER 41

"HOLD ON, EVERYONE!" Sheriff Mouton shouted as he approached the airfield. This wasn't the time to worry about destroying property. He rammed through the chain-linked gate, splitting it open.

"There he is," Sanders said, pointing at Johnson's hangar.

With the door open, the sheriff's hunch—and Sanders' too—proved correct. Johnson planned to fly out of the bayou and likely disappear. But that wasn't going to happen. Not in Sheriff Mouton's parish.

He parked the truck about fifty yards away from the hangar.

"If I were you, I'd go hide over there in the office. There's a key around back under the mat. Stay in there until this is over. Back up is supposed to be here soon but who knows how long that will be because of that wreck earlier." He paused. "How's that leg of yours?"

"It's only a flesh wound," Cal said.

Sheriff Mouton chuckled. "We'll make a bayou man out of you yet, city slicker. Now, get outta here."

He watched Sanders and Potter hustle through the rain to the office while Cal hobbled behind them.

"Nowhere to hide," he muttered to himself.

***

Johnson peered through the cockpit and onto the airstrip. He watched Cal, Potter and Sanders scurry to the office while Sheriff Mouton jammed clips into his handguns and loaded his rifle.

This isn't going to be easy.

He needed to create a diversion, something that would draw the sheriff out into the open so he could take a clear shot and give him the time he needed to get the plane airborne. He glanced around the hangar for an idea.

In the corner sat a four-wheel vehicle. He found a flare gun on a worktable.

This oughtta do the trick.

In the back of the structure was a set of double doors, wide enough for him to push the four wheelers through and to the corner of the hangar, just out of the sheriff's line of sight. He grabbed a few scraps of cloths and jimmied a way to hold the throttle open.

Then came a bullhorn announcement. "All right, Frank. Your little shenanigans are over. You need to surrender now," said Sheriff Mouton, who stood outside his truck and used the driver's side door as a shield.

He's an idiot if he thinks I'm going to surrender.

Johnson fired up the engine and let it warm up. Timing was critical. He still held the element of surprise. Sheriff Mouton remained transfixed on the jet in the hangar. Johnson smiled.

Here we go!

Johnson edged the barrel of the flare gun around the corner and aimed it at the sheriff. He pulled the trigger. Orange smoke created a visible plume against the dark sky and startled the sheriff, who began firing his gun at the flare. Then Johnson turned the four wheeler lose, sending it speeding across the runway.

Instead of directing the vehicle straight toward the sheriff, Johnson set a perpendicular trajectory. It drew Sheriff Mouton away from his driver's side door so he could get a better shot at it. The space and time was enough for Johnson to get a bead on him and take a shot with his rifle.

Take that!

Johnson looked through his scope to see the sheriff clutching his arm and blood spattered everywhere.

Adios, amigos!

He sprinted back toward the plane and made a few quick checks. He looked at the radar and plotted a course that would take him around the storm. His window to get his jet in the air thinned with each passing moment.

As he scurried around the hangar loading anything he deemed necessary into it, he looked back across the tarmac to see the sheriff still there writhing in pain. But he wasn't alone. Sanders knelt over him and applied pressure to his wound.

"What in the—" Johnson said. Sanders picked up the gun and was inspecting the chamber.

Johnson wasted no time in hustling back to the corner of the building and training his scope on Sanders. He put it squarely on Sanders' head.

Do it!

But he couldn't. Not the head. Gertie's words echoed in his head. He didn't need to kill anyone.

He fired a shot that ripped through Sanders' bicep and sent him sprawling to the ground.

He dashed back into the hangar, grabbed a few more

belongings, climbed aboard and secured the cabin door.

Time to fly!

He eased the jet through the hangar door and onto the runway.

***

Potter looked out the window at Sanders and the sheriff, both bleeding. "We've got to do somethin'," he said.

Sitting in a chair next to a window on the other side of the room, Cal nodded. He continued to record the action with his cell phone.

"There's not much I can do," Cal said as he gestured toward his leg. "I can't shoot a gun and I sure won't run anybody down in this condition. What's your bright idea?"

"You think that rifle is still loaded?"

"You can't be serious, Potter? I've seen you shoot, remember. Besides, if you weren't such a bad shot, I would've never come down here in the first place."

Potter didn't answer. He dashed out the door and toward the sheriff's truck.

***

"What now?" Johnson asked. He watched Potter scramble toward the sheriff and pick up his rifle. "Oh, this is rich."

He navigated the aircraft away from the truck and toward the far end of the airfield. Once he reached the end, he turned the jet around.

Then he laughed at the sight before him: Potter lying on his belly on the rain-soaked tarmac with a gun aimed at him.

"I like these odds!" he said to himself as he checked his flaps and eased the throttle forward.

CHAPTER 42

JAW SET, POTTER PRESSED his right eye against the scope of the rifle and steadied his aim. A few feet away, Sheriff Mouton applied pressure to his wound while he sat up against the back left tire of his truck. He ignored the deluge, unlike Sanders who huddled in the cabin as he tried to stop his bleeding.

"Where's my backup?" the sheriff groused.

Potter didn't flinch. "Right here," he said.

"I've seen you shoot, remember? We might as well go fill out an incident report and turn this over the feds."

"You got that much faith in me?"

The sheriff laughed. "Ever the optimist, Potter."

The jet engines roared as the plane began to rumble toward them.

"You're an LSU fan, right, Sheriff?" Potter asked.

"One of the biggest."

"You remember the Blue Grass Miracle?"

"How could I forget?"

"Did you believe they could comeback then and win that game?"

"No, but at least they had a chance with a strong-armed quarterback and speedy receivers. All we've got now is a guy

243

who couldn't hit the ocean with a rock while standing on the beach."

"But you've got a guy with a rock, Sheriff. Sometimes that's all you need."

Confident he had the shot he wanted, Potter eased his finger onto the trigger and pulled. The first crack from the gun ripped through the air, then several more followed.

Potter watched as the plane's front tire exploded from a direct hit. The jet began to teeter back and forth until one of the wings scraped the ground. Despite the drenched runway, sparks flew everywhere. The plane veered off the runway and toward the grass before it erupted into a fiery explosion. Dark plumes of smoke shot toward the sky.

He stood up and stared at the flames consuming the jet. Cal hobbled out of the office and stood next to Potter. He put his arm around the sharpshooter.

"Nice shot," Cal said.

After a moment, Potter started to run toward the plane.

"Where do you think you're going?" Sheriff Mouton yelled.

"I've gotta get Johnson outta there," Potter said.

"Don't. He's gone."

"But—"

"Just leave him alone. It's too dangerous."

Sirens wailed in the distance.

"Now they show up," the sheriff said. "Just in time to clean up this mess."

CHAPTER 43

THE TOULON PARISH SHERIFF'S Office bustled with activity. On the sidewalk just outside the office, several deputies spoke with witnesses.

"Are the desks all filled?" Sheiff Mouton asked.

"All but yours," one of the deputies replied.

The sheriff pushed his way through the doors and nearly bowled over several deputies blocking the major thoroughfare through the office.

"I ain't seen this place so busy since a couple of days after Hurricane Katrina," the sheriff said to Cal. Then to the rest of his entourage, "Follow me."

Sheriff Mouton led Cal, Potter and Hugh Sanders to his office and told them to take a seat. He shuffled behind his desk and sank into his chair.

He clasped his hands together and put them on his desk. "Does anyone want to tell me what you guys were really doing at Devil's Point tonight?" he asked.

All three of the men looked down and said nothing.

"I don't think you want me drawin' my own conclusions," he snapped.

Cal took a deep breath. "It wasn't a big deal."

"Wasn't a big deal? When I got there, I thought a gator

was muchin' on yer leg. And you're gonna tell me it wasn't a big deal?"

"I mean, nobody is going to be pressing charges, if that's what you're asking," Cal said.

"That's not what I'm askin'. I wanna know what happened."

Sanders cleared his throat. "It was my fault, sheriff. I took Cal here with me as bait to draw out Frank. We needed to make a trade."

"Took me as bait? That's a nice way of putting it," Cal snapped. "I wonder if shoving a burlap sack on someone's head and tossing them into the back of a pickup truck is how you take all your friends along for a ride somewhere."

Sheriff Mouton squinted and stared at Sanders. "Is this true?"

Sanders nodded. "I wasn't tryin' to hurt anybody. I didn't think Frank would go that far."

"Was he the one who threw Cal into the swamp?" the sheriff asked.

"Yep. And against my strong protests, I might add," Sanders said.

"Don't make yourself out like you tried to save the day," Cal said to Sanders. "You're not even close to being a saint, much less a hero."

"We all know who really saved your day, Cal," the sheriff said. "Now, what exactly was this trade about?"

"College football." Cal grew more disgusted at the situation once he uttered the words aloud. "Johnson and Sanders here were going to make a trade over some video tape that would sink Bryant's program."

"Was there anything explicit on the tape?" the sheriff asked. "I need to cover all my bases."

Cal shook his head. "No, but Sanders used me as insurance in a trade that ensured both these idiots got what they wanted."

"I doubt Johnson wanted what he got," the sheriff said.

"I didn't mean to kill him," Potter said.

The sheriff stood up and walked around to the front of his desk. He put his arm around Potter and squeezed him. "Tonight, you're the hero, Potter." He paused. "I know you didn't mean to kill him."

Potter walked back toward the sheriff. "I just wanted to stop him from taking off."

"I'm not talkin' about Johnson."

Potter froze. "What—what are you talkin' about?"

"You know exactly what I'm talkin' about. That huntin' accident, remember?"

"I wasn't tryin' to kill Tre'vell Baker," Potter said. Tears began to stream down his face. "I only meant to scare him a little. I don't know what I was thinking."

"You weren't thinkin', except about yer stupid college football," the sheriff said. "You were drunk on some fool's ideal. I know you didn't mean to kill 'em, but it's your cross to bear now. I had half a mind to throw you in prison earlier this week, but Lanette Baker told me she didn't want me dredging anything up unless it was murder—and I felt inclined to respect her wishes. It was stupid on your part, but it wasn't murder. A stupid accident, just like tonight. Anyway, I've thought it over and there ain't no use in ruinin' two people's lives over a momentary lapse in judgment." Then to Cal. "Ain't that right, Mr. City Slicker?"

Cal nodded.

"If I see this story of Tre'vell Baker's death appear in any book or article with your name on it—or anybody else's for that matter—I'll drag you back down here to the bayou and find somethin' to charge you with," the sheriff said. "You got that?"

Cal nodded again.

"However, tonight's tale is fair game. It's up to you how you want to spin it. But if you're gonna run around tellin' everybody that you got kidnapped by a crazy car salesman from Birmingham, you better tell me now if you want to press charges. Otherwise, I'll tell everybody my version of the truth."

Cal sighed and looked at Sanders. "I agree with you, sheriff. I think there have been enough people's lives ruined over this unfortunate event. And I believe Mr. Sanders here deserves the same level of grace you extended to Potter."

"Sounds good to me," the sheriff said. "And while I'm sure the people of Saint-Parran appreciate your patronage to our little parcel of earth in the bayou, I suggest you both stay away from here. Especially you, Sanders. I want your house on the market by Monday or else I'll be collecting a ridiculous-sized tax on your property from here on out. Understand?"

CHAPTER 44

THE STORM SPED UP but turned before it crashed ashore ahead of schedule Saturday morning, pounding the coast of Mississippi. The storm touched the fringes of Louisiana, causing some damage to Saint-Parran but not enough to earn a mention from the locals.

Cal needed to grab a cup of Louisiana's best coffee at Café Lagniappe one last time before he returned to Atlanta.

"Good mornin', Cal," Gertie said when he walked through the door. "I didn't think I'd see you here again."

"I didn't think I'd see anyone again after what happened last night." He sat down at the bar.

"You and me both." She placed a steaming cup of coffee in front of him.

"You heard about what happened to me at Devil's Point?"

She shook her head. "I was talkin' about myself."

"Did you get in an accident?"

"Worse. On my way home from work last night, Frank Johnson abducted me at gunpoint and forced me to drive him to the airfield."

"Oh, Gertie."

"I tried to talk some sense into him, but he wouldn't listen. And now the poor soul is dead."

Cal sipped his coffee. "I guess you heard about what happened later then?"

"Honey, you can't hardly pick your nose without it makin' the gossip rounds here."

"It was somethin' else, let me tell you."

"I look forward to readin' your article about it."

"I'm not looking forward to reliving that experience."

"I heard that."

Eager to move on, Cal changed the subject. "At least the storm missed Saint-Parran last night."

"Thank God for Mississippi," Gertie said with a hearty laugh. "They always find a way to make the rest of us look better—even when it comes to storms."

"I heard that." Cal smiled. "Thank you for all your talks over the past week and the best coffee I've ever had in Louisiana." He tossed a twenty-dollar bill on the counter and stood up to leave.

She leaned on the counter and took his hand, patting it affectionately. "You take care. Maybe we'll see you around here again sometime soon under better circumstances."

***

Cal's plane touched down at Hartsfield-Jackson Airport in Atlanta just before 2 p.m. Though he'd already called Kelly to tell her all about the excitement in the bayou, he couldn't wait to see her.

Before he took two steps through the door, she leaped into his arms and gave him a big hug.

"What was that for?" he asked.

"I was so worried about you," she said. "I'm just glad you're OK."

"It was quite an adventure."

"But everything is OK now, right? I mean, you're back in time to cover that Hawks' game for Gatlin, aren't you?"

Cal walked into the living room and slumped onto the couch. "Gatlin gave me the night off. And he thinks I've got all I need to write a compelling piece, but it's not all good news."

"Why's that?" Kelly sat down next to him and put her hand on his knee.

"I talked to that literary agent Mike Nicholson this morning and told him everything that happened."

"And?"

"He doesn't think there's a book there."

"What?" Kelly stared mouth agape. "How can there *not* be a book about this? It's got everything you could want."

"Unfortunately, it's got me."

"What do you mean?"

Cal leaned forward and ran his hands through his hair. "I'm too much a part of the story. He said it'd sound too self-serving if I told it."

"Couldn't someone else write it?"

"Yeah, but that kind of defeats the purpose, doesn't it?"

"It's still a great story."

"Yeah, but it's not a story that is going to get me a book deal so we can get that surgery you need."

"I'm not sure it matters any more."

"What are you saying?"

"I'm saying, we're pregnant!" Kelly pulled a pregnancy test stick out of her pocket and showed it to Cal. He stared in awe.

"Are you serious? Pregnant?"

Grinning, Kelly nodded. "Yes, I'm serious."

"How did this happen?"

"Seriously, Cal?"

"I mean, I didn't think you could get pregnant."

"I didn't either, but I don't think these things lie." Kelly pulled out three other pregnancy test sticks out of her pocket and slid them onto the coffee table.

"These are all positive?"

Kelly nodded. "Every one of them one."

"Well then, we're gonna have a baby!"

###

ACKNOWLEDGMENTS

EVER SINCE MY FIRST VISIT to Louisiana, I've always wanted to write a novel based on this unique slice of Americana. Despite my own experiences in that beautiful state over the years, this project wouldn't have achieved the depth I hoped for without the help of others who deserve recognition.

The Louisiana Sheriff's Association helped me craft an authentic representation of the unique duties of Louisiana sheriffs, which differ from most states.

Chip Towers from *The Atlanta Journal-Constitution* helped me track down several recruiting stories to enrich the characters.

Don Brown, who helped me years ago while investigating an NCAA violation case, came through again for me in sharing more exciting recruiting tales.

Kelly Morris from *The Times-Picayune* was more than gracious with her time in helping me make sure there was a level of authenticity around Louisiana high school football as portrayed in the book as well as a few other details about the state.

Jennifer Wolf once again helped make this a better story with her deft editing skills.

Dan Pitts crafted a beautiful cover that captures the mystery and wonder of where this novel took place.

Bill Cooper continues to crank out stellar audio versions of all my books — and I have no doubt that this will yield the same high-quality listening enjoyment.

As always, I must acknowledge my wife for her support in urging me on to keep writing.

And last but not least, without you, the reader, who have found my work—and enjoyed it—I never would have trudged on with the arduous task of writing more novels. Just knowing that you're all out there and enjoying the diversions created by my books continues to inspire me to press on and work diligently to refine my craft.

ABOUT THE AUTHOR

JACK PATTERSON is an award-winning writer living in southeastern Idaho. He first began his illustrious writing career as a sports journalist, recording his exploits on the soccer fields in England as a young boy. Then when his father told him that people would pay him to watch sports if he would write about what he saw, he went all in. He landed his first writing job at age 15 as a sports writer for a daily newspaper in Orangeburg, S.C. He later earned a degree in newspaper journalism from the University of Georgia, where he took a job covering high school sports for the award-winning *Athens Banner-Herald* and *Daily News*.

He later became the sports editor at a daily newspaper in south Georgia before working in the magazine world as an editor and freelance journalist. He has won numerous writing awards, including a national award for his investigative reporting on a sordid tale surrounding an NCAA investigation over the University of Georgia football program.

Jack enjoys the great outdoors of the Northwest while living there with his wife and three children. He still follows sports closely.

He also loves connecting with readers and would love to hear from you. To stay updated about future projects, connect with him over Facebook or on the Internet at www.IamJackPatterson.com

CPSIA information can be obtained at www.ICGtesting.com
Printed in the USA
LVOW11s1846070616

491604LV00004B/125/P